FRIGHTS FROM THE FORGE

A Collection of Terrifying Tales
BOOK ONE

a book by **Odd&Mollie** Supply LLC © 2026

Join our community, visit OddandMollie.com today for content & promotions.

STORYFORGE

STORYFORGE SERIES, Frights From the Forge Book 1, First Edition, 2026

All artwork and book layout by: **synsored**

FRIGHTS FROM THE FORGE

STORYFORGE was built for storytellers.

One image. Two text prompts. Endless possibilities.

Fragments of creative concepts designed to be used as tools for your imagination. Sparks meant to ignite, provoke and challenge your creativity, to continue these fleeting glimpses of worlds and characters where the prompt stops. Ultimately, we created something that we could not find on the shelves.

For years, our Horror volumes have offered those inspirations to storytellers. Tantalizing morsels for a ravenous mind, fragments of fear meant to be nurtured by your talent into a feast of artistry. But as you well know—imagination cannot be contained.

FRIGHTS FROM THE FORGE represents the maturation of that concept. We have allowed our authors to finish their thoughts. Each of the stories presented here was forged directly from prompts already published in our volumes of **STORYFORGE: Horror.**

From the minds of the very creators of the prompts themselves, we present the conclusions to their dark musings. Hand-picked by the authors and presented here to show the path a single spark can illuminate, and where that path might lead when followed to its darkest edge.

We hope you enjoy the following three hand-crafted stories, dedicated to our goal: to inspire writers to push their limits, their ideas and their comfort zones.

Thank you for being part of our community.⊛

The **STORYFORGE** Team.

STORYFORGE SERIES

TABLE OF CONTENTS

All the Quiet Things

Inspired by STORYFORGE: Advanced Horror Writing Prompts BOOK ONE

PROMPT OPTION 2:

Claire mourned her loss again as she prepared to exorcise the ghost; reminding herself this was not the friend she had known all her life, that person was gone, what remained had been twisted, but how, why?

ALL THE QUIET THINGS

DAY ONE ~ Wetherby-on-Stone

Clara Whitmore was alone. The thick, white cloud of steam billowed about her, dusting her porcelain skin with a feathery touch that turned cold in the autumn air. The young girl waited for it to part with an eagerness she could not suppress. What would its passage reveal? Would her world suddenly revert to normal? Would everything suddenly be set aright like waking from a bad dream.

The rumble of the train echoed in her chest as it pulled away, belching vapor with a long, drawn-out hiss. The pale shroud lifted revealing a sign on the narrow platform that read Wetherby-on-Stone. Standing before the sign was an older man, tall and thin who smelled of tobacco and peat. The stationmaster recognized Clara at once. Tall for her age with pale skin and bright-blue eyes. Dark hair neatly braided over one shoulder, just like the picture in the broadsheets.

The man suddenly grew awkward, avoiding Clara's gaze. She understood; there was nothing the man could say or do to ease her pain. But the reaction did make her loneliness sting all that much more. Whenever Clara thought about being alone, it had been a solitary experience. Now she felt alone while among other people, and it was not an experience she had ever imagined.

"Good morning, little one," the man looked curiously at her too-large coat. It wasn't Clara's coat. She had lost hers somewhere, she didn't remember. Didn't care.

Daddy's lawyer had cared. He had put her in his coat at the station so she would be warm. A kind gesture to be sure, but the

Clara Whitmore

young girl only saw the bared teeth and glaring looks from those around her. Why did you live, and so many better die?

Clara understood this reaction as well. She wondered the same thing.

"Where is your luggage, girl." He looked around, fearing it might have remained on the train.

She held up a worn satchel, the leather had paled and begun to crack along the seams. The travel bag contained a few clothes, she would receive her uniforms when she arrived at school, and other sundries including some worn books and a dry sandwich the secretary had given her for the trip. It remained intact as Clara was rarely hungry these days.

He pointed a thick, sooty finger toward a small, overgrown cart path. "Wetherby's that way, not far. Stay on the path and you'll find it. And smile, girl, it can't be as bad as all that."

The last part reminded Clara of something her father used to say, but she pushed the memories down. She would not mourn in front of a stranger. Besides, she had grown weary of mourning. Without another word the stationmaster walked away leaving her staring at the path that led into the mist-bound hills.

Apparently, there would be no one from the school to meet her. As there had been no porter to help her down, no carriage waiting at the gate. Her left hand dropped to her side, feeling for the hard, oval shape in her pocket beneath the ill-fitting coat. An action that was quickly becoming an unconscious habit.

Clara pulled her hand back quickly.

She didn't want to deal with that now, just needed to confirm it was still with her.

Clara stood there for a moment, unsure whether the sudden tightness in her chest was from anticipation or the crisp air. Then she began to walk. The woods were still, and silence hung over the autumn forest. The sort of quiet that stood out in nature as unnatural.

The road to Wetherby Girls' Academy snaked upward through thickets of thorn and ash, the sort of English countryside that never truly felt tamed. Moss spilled down low stone walls that kept her on the path. The school was a mile off, perhaps more, concealed up the rising road and behind more trees. Somehow Clara could feel it already, waiting.

The dull grey skies felt oppressive and wore on her already depressed mind. The cold bit her skin anywhere it found a way past her coat, and her nose had gone numb already. Clara had thought the train was cold, but it paled in comparison to the late fall countryside.

The amber was strangely warm in her inner pocket. It always was, no matter what the weather or where she kept it. That, among other things, frightened her. But they had come through a tragedy together, and while Clara wasn't quite sure what that meant, she did understand that it meant something.

And right now, Clara had nothing.

Up ahead, the gates came into view.

Tall wrought-iron bars, flaked with rust and grime. Dried leaves swirled and gathered about the metal base. One of the gate's doors hung open just wide enough to allow the willowy girl to pass through. Only the thin outline of Wetherby lay beyond, its stone spires rising into view above the fog. Clara paused at the threshold.

Beyond the gates, the gravel path narrowed. Trees lined the way, bare-limbed and motionless despite the wind that pressed at her back like an encouraging hand. Somewhere in the branches, a bird called out, sharp and solitary. Scandalous in the silence.

Clara stepped through.

A chill ran through her body as she crossed the threshold, either from the bleak atmosphere, or some premonition. Clara did not like this place. But that didn't matter, she had no other option, so she forced herself onward.

The neglected path swallowed the sound of her footsteps and the mist thickened. It curled around her boots and fingers and throat. The uneven ground took its toll and her pace slowed at times. Her breath came fast now, clouding the air in front of her, but she kept walking, jaw tight, spine straight.

A little part of Clara felt she deserved some neglect.

The Wetherby Academy for Girls

The front doors loomed over Clara; the double oaken slabs fitted with black iron hinges and a lion-headed knocker that looked too heavy to lift. She ignored it and instead tried the smaller brass latch and found the door already unlatched, creaking open upon her touch. The cloying odor of old things rushed out to meet her. Old ink, scorched tea, drying leather.

As Clara crossed the threshold, she felt something akin to a spider's web across her face. She reached up to clean it from her eyes and nose, but nothing seemed to be there. She turned in place and checked herself for eight-legged stowaways but found no spiders on her coat. Clara tallied it up to imagination and entered the building.

The entrance hall rose in a hollow arch overhead, timbered with thick beams and hung with a faded banner: Disciplinæ Fidelis— Faithful to Discipline. The air was dry and cold, the kind that stole moisture from your lungs.

Clara stepped inside, her boots echoing sharply in the grand entrance. She shouldered the giant door closed. Then, from a corridor that led to her left, voices—muffled, girlish. A door slammed, cutting off the laughter. Then a woman approached from the hall to her right.

The lean woman glided toward Clara with such rigid posture she reminded Clara of a puppet on wires. Her dress was black serge, her collar white and starched into submission and accessorized with a brooch at the throat. Dark umber hair was styled with precision, swept up and away from her face in a voluminous Edwardian coiffure.

Miss Albin

"Whitmore," the woman said. It was not a question. Round spectacles framed her intelligent eyes and her expression declared that she would not tolerate nonsense.

"Yes, ma'am," Clara replied, standing straighter.

"I am Miss Albin. Mathematics mistress. You are expected. Follow me. Quietly, please."

Miss Albin turned and began walking without waiting for acknowledgment. Clara hurried to follow, her satchel bumping against her hip. The corridors of Wetherby were narrow and unlit except by the pallid spill of light from tall arched windows. The stillness lay thick in the ancient halls, and the girl did her best to respect it; any sound felt invasive here.

They passed a sitting room where a fire crackled weakly in the hearth. Several girls sat on high-backed chairs, knitting or reading. All heads lifted to watch when Clara passed. One girl with heavy-lidded eyes whispered behind her hand. The rest simply stared.

None of them smiled.

Miss Albin led her to a small study. A brass plate on the door read 'GOVERNESS'. The woman within was tall, poised, and composed. Her posture remained straight despite the wear of age, suggesting a lifetime of discipline and earned authority. Her expression was neither stern nor soft, but somewhere between the two; a quiet strength laced with experience. Her grey hair was scraped back into a bun, and she wore a high-necked blouse and skirt, the ensemble practical yet elegant in its Edwardian austerity. The subtle ruffle at her throat hinted at a formality that never strayed into vanity.

"Thank you, Miss Albin," the Governess said as both an acknowledgment and a dismissal.

Miss Albin flashed Clara a brief smile before turning and walking out of the study.

"Hello, Clara. My name is Miss Florence Lawson; I will be your Governess here at Wetherby. We're all very sorry for what you have gone through." Her eyes conveyed feeling, and Clara believed her. Though in truth, it offered her no comfort.

"Thank you," the girl replied from habit.

"Follow me," Miss Lawson led Clara from the study. "You're assigned to Dormitory C, South Wing, here is a slate with your class schedule."

They made their way up a large stairway to the second floor.

"Theresa Bellamy is the senior girl for your Dormitory, she will instruct you concerning all you need to know, where to go, and how to get there. You can ask her any questions that you have."

"I understand," Clara replied.

"Lunch is in a few minutes," she stopped at the doorway and motioned with one hand for Clara to enter. "You just have enough time to freshen up. Welcome to Wetherby, Clara. If you need anything, come to me."

"Thank you," Clara forced a smile.

The door to the room was half-open. Inside, six girls were seated on narrow beds, their boots lined neatly beneath. Rows of empty beds lined both walls, but the six girls had chosen beds clustered around the fireplace. All of them looked at

her, then quickly looked away. Clara wasn't surprised that her scandal had preceded her.

"So, you're the ship girl," someone said, not unkindly. "I'm Theresa Bellamy."

Clara turned toward the speaker. She was older than the others with thick, dark tresses that were barely constrained by pins. The dark hair contrasted with a face of sculpted ivory skin, well-defined brows, and lips the color of drying rose petals. She had the look of someone used to being watched.

Dressed in the formal, high-collared uniform of the girls' academy, her blouse was finely detailed with ruffles and a row of delicate buttons, the pleated skirt falling in impeccable lines that hinted at discipline and order.

"Why didn't you drown?"

That came from a different voice near the windows. Flat. Curious, and not kind. A lament more than a question.

Another older girl stood there; she leaned to one side running a brush through honey-brown hair. Her eyes were locked firmly on Clara.

The other girls fell quiet.

Clara felt the weight of their stares. The weight of their judgment. Of her guilt.

"I don't know," she said, simply.

"Cecily Pembroke," Theresa said by way of introduction, "and she's not going to ask any more questions."

Theresa Bellamy

Cecily
Pembroke

Lottie
Dunn

Joanna
Mills

The statement had teeth, and the two older girls stared each other down for a long, silent moment. Cecily shrugged and tossed the hairbrush on her bed as she passed by on her way out of the room. She made one last stop by Clara.

"That's a nice coat," her lips twisted in a wry smile, "you should try a woman's fit sometime."

Theresa resumed her introductions after the other girl had left.

"This is Lottie Dunn."

Lottie wore a sneer on her pale face, otherwise she might have been pretty. She was older, with rich, brown hair that flowed down her shoulders unrestrained. Without a word or wave of greeting, Lottie bounced out of her bed and followed Cecily out of the dormitory.

Theresa ignored her churlishness and moved on.

"This is Joanna Mills," she indicated a young girl, maybe eight or nine years old. Her dark eyes were wide and alert, framed by thick, chestnut hair that cascaded in loose waves nearly down to her waist. It was carefully parted and brushed, though slightly tousled as though she'd come in from a windblown walk between dormitory and classroom. The long curls framed a heart-shaped face with delicate features.

Joanna raised a delicate hand and waved at Clara.

"This is Mabel Finch."

Her porcelain skin and delicate features were wreathed by a mane of pale, flaxen hair that flowed in loose, natural waves just past the girl's shoulders. Wide blue-grey eyes watched her from

behind round spectacles that had to have been intended for an adult's face.

Mabel added a weak smile to her wave.

Theresa pivoted to the other side of the room and motioned to another girl sitting cross-legged on a bed.

"This is Ada Bello."

Her hair was a deep ash-blonde, braided into a long, slightly untidy plait that fell over one shoulder. Her face was pale and clear, her gaze direct and calculating. There was a thoughtful stillness in her eyes that made Clara uncomfortable. She again forced a smile in response to a half-hearted welcome.

"And finally, this is Maisie Long."

The girl's pale complexion was offset by a cascade of light brown hair, parted at the center and tumbling in soft waves over her shoulders. She was younger than Clara by a few years. But her eyes, wide and unblinking behind round spectacles sparkled with intelligence. Maisie offered a wide smile, and promptly began scratching away in a small, leather-bound diary.

Clara's mother had encouraged her to keep a diary, but Clara had never felt drawn to the activity. She also got the distinct impression that Maisie might be the one that records events for the teachers, and delights in the telling.

The senior girl pointed to an empty bed beside Maisie's, "and this is your bed."

Theresa turned to address the remaining girls.

Maisie Long

She said, "Bells in five minutes," then moved closer to Clara and lowered her voice. "You'll want to wash your face. You look grey."

Clara stepped up to the bed that was to be hers and set her satchel down carefully. The blanket was rough wool. The pillow was firm and thin. Someone had left a pair of socks beneath it—worn and wadded. Deliberately, no doubt.

She didn't bother to move them; it was a weak prank from a weak mind.

Instead, she sat, clasped her hands, and listened as the girls filed out one by one, their laughter returning once her back was turned. The wind outside the window scraped at the glass like fingernails reminding her she was trapped. Abandoned in the English hinterlands by people who didn't care, surrounded by others that hated her for being a victim of a war she barely understood.

The Dining Hall

The bell clanged twice, the first note fell flat, the second one ringing out through the halls. Clara followed the procession of boots and black stockings down the corridor, trying not to brush against anyone. The other girls moved in orderly pairs, talking in clipped voices or not at all. Laughter, when it came, was brief and private. They passed through a set of heavy doors into the dining hall, and the vastness of the hall gave the hush a weight she could feel pressing on her shoulders.

Long wooden tables filled the room in neat rows. Oil lamps hung low from iron hooks above, casting dim puddles of gold across the scarred wooden surfaces. The windows, tall and narrow, were clouded with condensation and everything smelled faintly of boiled beef and floor polish. Girls filed in by year. Clara hesitated near the threshold until someone nudged her from behind.

"Go on, ship girl," came a voice, half-joke, half-not.

Clara found a place at the edge of a bench, neither at the head nor the foot of the table. She kept her hands in her lap as others sat, backs straight, eyes forward. Bowls were already waiting, half-filled with stew: thin gravy, chunks of carrot, and stringy meat that clung to bone.

Seated across from her sat Mabel Finch, the quiet girl with the too-large spectacles. She gave Clara a small, nervous glance, then looked quickly away as though she had violated some tenant. To her left, Lottie Dunn slid in, sharp-eyed and smirking, a bandage on one finger.

"Are you not a fan of soup?" She asked no one in particular. "I'm

Mabel Finch

sure they can whip up some saltwater for you?"

There were a few stifled laughs. Not cruel, but not kind, either.

Clara said nothing.

From the head of the table, Theresa Bellamy raised her spoon. Every motion she made was careful and poised. She hadn't spoken since the dormitory, but her eyes found Clara now, unreadable and dark. She didn't smile. It was a test.

The girls around her waited. And when Theresa began to eat, they all did.

Clara lifted her spoon, her hand steady despite the murmurs. She tasted the broth, sour and too hot. She didn't eat any more of the stew, it tasted like saltwater. Silence hung thickly over the table.

And then a soft clatter.

A bowl had been pushed forward. Theresa from the head of the table was looking directly at Clara.

"Hands on the table, Whitmore," she said, not unkindly, but as one correcting a student. "We don't hunch like factory children."

More laughter, this time nervous.

Clara raised her chin. She did as she was told. Slowly. Deliberately. Not defiantly, just a dash of rebellion. Theresa watched Clara a moment longer. Then she turned her attention back to her own bowl.

The tension broke with the scrape of spoons and the resumed murmur of talk.

Across from her, Mabel whispered without looking up, "They'll get bored eventually."

Clara didn't respond. She'd been stared at before. Picked apart by strangers in borrowed rooms. This was no different. No worse. She took another look at her stew and sighed deeply. This was going to be a long school year.

Restless Night

Clara didn't sleep that night. Not because she didn't try, but her mind was assaulted by grief and the knowledge that sleep brought the dreams. The nightmares. The memories of her ordeal stirred together with copious glimpses from her life before, all reminding her of everything she had lost.

She had spent her free time the previous day getting her uniforms and storing them neatly in the trunk at the end of her bed. The big box had a lock, but there was no key in it, and no one provided one. She considered asking, she wanted to protect her amber jewel, but she doubted there would be any true safety at the foot of her bed.

No, she needed to always keep it on her person. There were very few things left in this world that belonged to her, and Clara wasn't going to give up any more of them. She spent the rest of her time exploring the school. She found the chapel, but it was a small affair and always seemed to be occupied when she passed.

So, she made her way to the third floor, a place strictly off limits for the students. It was perfect if it was a bit dark and dusty. But she was alone. She discovered several old classrooms and offices, most of them locked. Another room labeled with a handwritten sign read Records Office *No Admittance: Keep Locked at All Times.* The lock on the door was broken so Clara spent a few minutes confirming that the room held nothing of interest to her.

But out the tall arching windows she saw an old chapel and a small family cemetery. She could not assess the extent of the building's ruin from here but decided to find out in the morning. She hoped the sanctuary was still intact. Clara would much rather spend her time alone in a chapel than the dark and creepy back hallways of the school.

Clara found spending time in the dormitory unpleasant. They weren't all bad. But Cecily and Lottie made up for those who didn't torment her. It did not truly harm Clara, her parents had raised her better than that. The girl took none of their offenses to heart, but still, it was trying.

She felt the amber, unnaturally warm against her chest as she lay sleeplessly in her bed. She longed to take it out and feel its warmth against her skin. She longed to understand the strange relic that was forced upon her by a dying man while the ship she was on was sinking into the warm saltwater. And why she felt that she should have abandoned it.

Instead, it stayed with her. A bright, mysterious presence in the dark of every train car, the hollow of every station. When she closed her eyes, she could still feel the deck beneath her feet tilting, see the gold glint of the gemstone even in blackness. Amber with a face in it. A girl's face, finely etched and ancient as grief.

The girl was amazed that it was still on her person after she was rescued. Clara honestly had not understood the man's actions or the words he tried to say from his ruined mouth. In her nightmares he said it repeatedly, she felt the gravity of his earnestness, just as she had that day on the tilting deck of the ship. She had not understood him, however, not then nor in her dreams that came later.

And she dared not remove it to examine it where anyone else could see it. Also, and this confused her, she was a little scared of it. It was clearly not a normal stone, and she could swear that it had tried to talk to her.

Clara dismissed this thought as it passed through her mind. The last thing she needed was to be found mentally infirm.

What would daddy's lawyers do then?

Lock her up and take her family's wealth for their own?

And so, Clara had a new fear that would keep her awake at night.

Loss

The office of Headmistress Miss Eileen Anne Ebsworth was a room of austerity.

Stone-flagged and windowless, tucked like a secret into the western wing beneath the bell tower, she had no use for comfort. The furniture was hard-edged and well-oiled. Books stood in ranked formation behind glass. A single coal fire guttered in the grate, lighted more for form than any need for warmth.

She was dressed in a tailored, dark ensemble that reflected both propriety and understated elegance. Her jacket, cut close to the form, was fastened with a neat row of brass buttons. Beneath that, a high-collared blouse adorned with an intricate lace neck piece peeked out, fastened at the throat with a mustard-colored silk cravat that added a single, deliberate flash of color. Her long, pleated skirt flowed crisply to her ankles, the cut both dignified and practical.

The lamp on her desk was lit, though its light seemed unable to expel the dark from the corners. Her spectacles lay beside the inkwell. Her coat hung on its peg. Her shoes, polished to a mirror finish, rested side by side beneath her chair.

Order, in all things.

The Headmistress sat at her desk now, spine straight as a bayonet, hands flat on the desk holding down the broadsheet. Its headline blazoned in bold, dark ink across the top of the news-sheet; *SS Persia Torpedoed Off Crete Coast.* The printed words were burned into her memory. When she closed her eyes she saw them still, hanging before her in the darkness.

Headmistress
Ebsworth

The girls at Wetherby Girls' Academy were not just her wards; they were her legacy. Every one of them. Small, mercurial charges entrusted to her from all over the Empire. From grieving relatives to disinterested parents, survivors of epidemics and distant war fronts. Her personal feelings should not matter. Could not matter.

If they did, for any reason, then she will have failed as an educator.

Eileen accepted them, and in turn demanded from them the best of their character, even if she had to extract it herself. She was not cruel, nor was she unjust. She was precise.

But today, something scratched and worried at her edges. Inside her something coiled. A soft flex just behind her ribs, a second pulse that did not belong.

Clara Whitmore.

A girl, one of the few survivors, plucked from the sea like driftwood. Her family lost, but their privileged legacy lived on, and Clara was placed here by the tangled strings of money and grief and quiet panic. Everyone had the best of intentions, but no one knew how to help the poor girl. And Clara Whitmore deserved to be helped, Eileen reminded herself.

But Eleanor Thornton was dead.

Her grief rose again, unbidden, curling through her mind like a virulent infection. Eleanor—unflappable and brave, tragic and beautiful. The single greatest muse of modernism, at least in Eileen's humble opinion. The sleek silver figure that flew on the bonnets of cars, head lifted skyward, arms flung back in triumph.

Dead in the same sinking. Lost while Clara lived.

Eileen had nearly drowned when she was young and remained traumatized ever since. It wasn't just the sounds and images from that day that replayed in her mind. She could still feel the event as if it had just happened. The fire in her lungs, the weight in her legs that slowly increased as fighting for her life drained her of energy. The anguish that washed over her as she realized she was about to die.

She squeezed her eyes shut as the thoughts of her idol's final moments flashed unbidden across her mind's eye. She felt that pain again, though for someone else. Still, the wound was opened and only time would close it again.

Eleanor Thornton had helped Eileen through that time of her life. As an idol and role model the woman had been pivotal in shaping the young woman's path to come. She instilled confidence when it flagged, and determination when hers had waned.

Eileen had admired her from a distance of course, often holding her own life up to compare. Of course she lost, but she never minded losing to Eleanor. She admired the woman not as the world did—an ornament, a graceful flourish of art nouveau—but as a woman of ambition, of drive and quiet depth. A woman who made a difference.

And Clara?

What had she done? Lived. Watched helplessly as the sea took all the better of humanity and left her. The girl must have felt so lucky. Her fists clenched at the thought.

The headmistress's jaw tightened. She stood abruptly and

crossed the room to the fire. The coals had burned down to faint orange ribs beneath the black grate. Seizing the poker from habit she stirred the fading coals absently, her mind far from the task.

This is not you.

Was that true?

Eileen believed that all life could be broken down into numbers, therefore numbers had their own justification. But how much could she justify? Hating a child? An orphan? One who had literally swam the same path as her?

Her eyes drifted to the row of spirits lined up on the mantelshelf. Gifts from grateful alumni and parents. Many of the bottles were here before she took over the school. Eileen had never been a drinker but one didn't need to be to understand why souls in pain sought it out.

And Eileen was in pain.

Pleasant Dreams

Mary Barstow enjoyed her dream. That had been so rare since her arrival at the academy. Everything at Wetherby seemed to be constructed of greys and browns. Mary was convinced this place pulled the vitality from you if you stood still too long. But this dream was a welcome distraction.

The ballroom was white, brilliant white. And the colors of the gowns of the women were vivid splashes of color on the canvas. Light twinkled from precious metals and stones that adorned the dancers. Her own rich, windswept volume of auburn hair was braided into a delicate crown of pink crystal.

The rest of her slender body was wrapped in dark rose silk that made her stand out among the dancers. Her gown adhered to Edwardian propriety while suggesting something modern in its sharp silhouette. It enhanced her sexuality, or so she felt. The gown was familiar, like something she had designed herself in a previous life.

She was surrounded by beauty and light and warmth. The music was hypnotic, especially when combined with the rapid but steady movement of the other dancers. They circled her in pairs, spinning all the while, creating a sea of vibrant, changing colors in motion. Out of that chaos emerged a pattern in the coloring that caught her eye and pulled something from deep within her mind that tickled her body deep in the bone.

Then she was swept up by another dancer in a dark suit. The world was spinning about her. Mary was delighted. And her breath was stolen for a very different reason.

Mary
Barstow

The man she danced with, a prince to be sure, was tall and lean, his features concealed by a mask of plain porcelain. He was strong but agile. She didn't feel pinned in his grasp, but rather cradled. He charmed her without words.

It occurred to Mary that he was the only person wearing a mask, but the tides of the dream carried away such trivialities. His technique was exact, unrelenting. Soon she found herself out of breath keeping up. She felt a long-forgotten thrill, a stirring deep inside.

The crown upon his head was more substantial than hers. A thick, gold band burnished to a blinding finish. It widened above his brow to accommodate a great amber jewel that fascinated her. She could see herself in that stone, her future, her dreams. All coming true.

Yes, Mary enjoyed this dream very much.

DAY 2 ~ The Ruined Chapel

It took Clara nearly half an hour to locate a navigable path through the overgrown estate to the old chapel. There was no real path, just the faint memory of one, swallowed by moss and nettles, half-hidden behind a broken wall beyond the orchard. The girls at Wetherby had spoken of it in whispers, with the kind of superstitious relish reserved for stories told by candlelight: someone saw a face through the bell tower window, a voice sobbing in the rafters, scratches on the inside of the door.

Ghost stories told the night before by the older girls in the dormitory. Ghost stories didn't scare Clara. Not anymore.

Clara believed in death. She had met it face-to-face in the salty, oil-laden water of the Mediterranean. Ghosts, she wasn't so sure about. And it brought up the depressing thought of her family's spirits trapped in the wreckage at the bottom of that great sea. She forced that thought from her mind.

The chapel was older than the school by hundreds of years. The evidence could be seen clearly in the stones: smoothed at the edges by time and wind, veined with lichen and thin cracks. A partial roof remained, sunk on one side and open to the sky on the other. What windows hadn't been smashed stood empty, their glass lost long ago. Ivy poured through them like water through broken teeth.

Clara paused at the arch of the door frame. No door. No barrier, save silence itself.

She stepped inside.

The air in the chapel was warmer than outside, thick with damp earth and the quiet rot of leaves. It conferred the scent of old wood and wet cloth. Of secrets laid bare then hidden again by time. It seemed quieter inside, but then Clara found all chapels to have that in common. Above her, dust motes danced among the timbers of the broken roof, barely illuminated in the weak, pallid light of the overcast skies.

At the far end stood the remains of an altar, its base half-collapsed, the top crusted with droppings and moss. Wooden pews, scattered and broken, lined the floor like ribs from a great skeleton. Even in the current state of disrepair, it felt like a sanctuary from the academy.

Clara picked her way carefully between the wooden bones, her boots silent on the wet stone. Her breath formed little clouds in the cold air. She slipped off her satchel and sat on a block of carved stone that might once have held candles or icons. Her feet rested on a raised flagstone so old the writing carved on it had weathered so badly only an 'O' remained.

The moment she sat, exhaustion caught up with her. Last night she was certain she would be awake for days, but since early this morning she had been fighting to stay awake. Ms. Barstow had been particularly trying. The woman sat and read her favorite poetry to the girls. Clara had to resort to digging her nails into her palms to remain awake.

Now her palms hurt, and the rest of her body vibrated inside with nervous energy. She felt like her legs were melting into the stone as her weariness increased with inactivity. She wondered how life could go so askew, and that brought a wave of grief over her.

Clara sobbed quietly. The curiosity of the ghost stories forgotten in her pain. She didn't notice the dust motes in the ceiling high above had begun to move in unison. Circling in a ring above her.

Dreams In Darkness

That night, the dormitory creaked in its joints as the remorseless wind curled under the slates. Rain whispered against the tall windows in long, patient strokes. Across the room the younger girls were quizzing the seniors about the details of the ghost in the stories. To Clara's amusement and the frustration of the other girls, Mabel seemed determined to poke holes in every story and witness report the seniors offered up.

Deciding that Mabel was a wet blanket, Lottie suggested that they simply stop talking to her. But the shunning didn't seem to impress the tenacious little blonde. She showed no hurt in response but simply went silent, still listening to every word the others said.

Clara laid down. Her body felt like it melted into the bed as her exhaustion finally overwhelmed her. She felt herself sinking, no it was more like being pulled down. Under. Her mind panicked as she realized what was coming.

The amber gemstone had slipped from her pocket and lay beneath her hip. A soft, warm pulse that saw her off to her nightmares.

It began with the cold. Not the kind that prickles the skin, but the kind that settles into your heart. That curls inside you and waits for the inevitable tragedy. Dread.

Then came the sound. Not the screaming. Not the splintering wood. A crack, deep and final as if the ship's spine had been broken. It reverberated through the hull and traveled up her body.

This was not an accurate enactment of what had taken place that day, Clara had been knocked off her feet when the torpedo struck. Her dream recast her in the drama as an observer of the horrific events of that moment. Things she had seen and heard but ignored by her conscious mind due to adrenaline and shock.

Guilt showed her these horrors again in her nightmares every night. And always in new and creative torments.

The Persia groaned and popped beneath her feet. The deck tilted suddenly as the ship listed hard to port. She watched all the people gathered on deck for lunch in the Mediterranean sun slide down the deck and slam into the rail. The first casualties of the disaster were crushed beneath falling passengers and furniture.

It was over so fast, and yet it lasted so long. Seven minutes was all the time it took for the great liner to slip beneath the oily surface of the sea, taking hundreds of people to their watery grave. Including Clara's family.

Panicked people began a stampede. Voices shouted and cursed in English, French and Farsi. Trays shattered on the deck causing more chaos as the terrified passengers stumbled and fell on the debris.

The sea rose and smoke bloomed sideways. The sun vanished beneath billowing clouds of oily black smoke. Clara stood frozen, this was the part she hated the most.

The ship heaved over plunging the deck fully underwater. But Clara remained fixed to the ship's deck, watching the surreal scene as smoke and sky spun suddenly and stopped under water. From the deck, Clara saw a cloud of heavier bodies and debris began falling toward the sea bottom ahead of the Persia. The burning oil on the surface of the water cast a flickering, lambent light on the wreckage below.

Then he was there.

A man floated to her. Young, bloodied, bare to the waist. His face was half-burned, his mouth moving too fast to form real words. He grabbed her.

Not hard, not rough—urgent.

The memory was out of time and place. This had happened before the ship capsized, but in her nightmares, he always approached her after. Even under water, everything else played out the same. She could hear his rough voice, smell his cooked flesh.

He shoved something against her chest, fingers trembling as he pushed it between the folds of her blouse, inside, against her skin. She gasped at the contact, it burned her skin, but his grip was gone before she could cry out.

He breathed words into her ear, it was barely a voice at all. As in all of her dreams, should couldn't understand his plea. Then he slipped backward into the crush of bodies and debris and vanished.

But here, in her dreams, Clara refused the amber gemstone. She dropped it into the inky depths of the sea. A golden star that sank slowly into darkness. She felt right doing this, but suddenly she was sinking to the bottom like the others. And drowning.

The gemstone punished her for her disloyalty. All she had to do was accept the stone, but she refused. What ensued were weeks of constant nightmares, but instead of breaking down Clara, they had only reinforced her belief that the amber jewel was as dangerous as it was alluring.

In her dream she understood the stone was punishing her for refusing it. But by morning, that conviction would be a hazy memory.

She swam as hard as she could to escape from the sinking wreck above, but it was in vain. The Persia was too large. And Clara was too tired.

She was pinned beneath the wreck, her small body driven deep into the mud of the sea floor. In claustrophobic darkness Clara fought with all her might against an unmovable object. Her lungs caught fire, and she realized she was about to die.

Then she heard her father's voice; *Now surely, it's not as bad as all that.*

His deep timbre woke her from the nightmare with a jerk. It took a few moments for the last vestiges of the dream to wash from her mind. Then she recalled her father's voice. Grief overwhelmed her and she put her hands over her face and sobbed.

Clara cried as quietly as she could manage. She didn't want to wake the others. She didn't want the other girls to find any chink in her armor.

Mabel heard Clara crying and paused in her own weeping to listen to Clara's pain. And when Mabel finally fell asleep that night, she didn't feel quite so alone.

Waking

It was not a waking, but a stirring. Not an insignificant distinction considering the nature of the thing that slept beneath the ancient hill. A limited response to stimuli that allowed for finite reasoning without fully waking. This response helped to compensate for the protracted time it took for the creature to truly wake and thereby defray or prevent some of the energy consumed by that response.

If it was forced to wake, then it would need to feed. Truly feed.

It had sensed the entity in the when it first trespassed. It recognized the entity's kind. Several had passed above over the long years inhabiting the body of a human or animal. These interlopers never remained long and were more of a nuisance than threat. The creature was not in danger.

It was never in danger. Ever.

Some time passed, a flicker for the creature, and it was disturbed again. The entity remained among the humans above and had begun to feed. The trickling nourishment of suffering and strife that wept from the living above and sustained the creature in its hibernating state. It could allow nothing to interfere with its food supply; this was primal.

Food restriction escalated the response.

All other concerns were rescinded.

The creature began to wake.

DAY 3 ~ Influx

The morning came grey and shapeless, stitched together by fog and faint drizzle. The windowpanes in Dormitory C were veiled with condensation, the outlines of trees beyond diminished to little more than smudged shadows. Rain tapped softly on the glass.

Clara sat on the edge of her narrow bed, half-laced boots on the floor, blouse still damp at the collar. Around her, the dormitory stirred to life. Blankets were folded, stockings pulled, water splashed into tin basins.

She hadn't spoken. Not to anyone. Not even to herself. She had kept the dream and her grief inside her like a secret swallowed poorly that threatened to resurface at any moment. How could she share something like that with anyone?

She reached for the familiar warmth of the gemstone and realized it was missing. She stood quickly, her eyes scanning the small bed. She found it lying at the center of the mattress on the white sheets.

Then, from a few beds over, a voice broke the quiet.

"I had the best dream last night," said Ada.

"Let me guess," Cecily interrupted, "*your* ship sank but *your* family lived?"

Everyone went still.

The comment stung, but that wasn't Clara's chief concern at that moment. She had just laid her left hand over the gemstone and now all the girls in the dormitory were looking right at her.

"That's so funny, Cecily," Theresa commented dryly, "I'll have to share your joke with the Governess, I'm sure she'll find it very amusing too."

Cecily turned her back on the rest of them as she dressed. The distraction gave Clara enough time to pull the blanket over her hand and the gemstone.

"No," Ada continued, wisely avoiding the scuffle between the older girls. "It was my birthday, which is in only a few months, and I received a magic jewel that spoke to me."

Clara was surreptitiously sliding the gemstone out from under the blanket when she heard the girl's words and froze. What were the chances it was a coincidence?

"I found a pretty golden rock in my dream too," Maisie said.

Sweat formed on Clara's back.

"Oh, sure you did Maisie," Ada waved away the girl's comment, "you always have to worm your way into someone else's story."

Clara did not dismiss the younger dreamer's claim. She knew that the stone entered her own dreams at night. As insane as that sounded, she knew it to be true, but had assumed that her personal contact with the gemstone had allowed such a strange occurrence. But if it could reach out, touch other minds from a distance; how could she control that? How could she protect others from its seductive pull?

What fate had she brought to the Academy, and everyone that lived there. The dreams seemed to be bright and happy, not nightmares like her own. Still, a part of her worried about what would come of it.

Clara knew she should dispose of the gemstone. Either give it away or toss it deep into the thicket near the orchard. But every time she thought about tossing the stone away, she remembered all they had been through together. That counted for something. Didn't it?

In a way, it was one of the few things left in this world that was hers. Not gifted from sympathetic souls who tried to bury her grief in gifts. Nor was it purchased out of duty by her father's lawyers. No, the gemstone was hers, and they had survived together.

This was too much for Clara to deal with now. First things first; she needed a better hiding place for the gemstone. But it felt riskier not having it on her person. She knew more about the amber than anyone else at the academy. And while what knowledge she had amounted to very little, Clara still felt responsible. After all, she had brought the gemstone into the school, and into the lives of everyone at the academy.

Her eye fell on the small sewing kit her mother had bought her just before they boarded the liner. Clara wasn't an accomplished seamstress, but she had been taught. Surely, she could sew a hidden pocket into her clothes to hide the stone.

A bell clanged somewhere downstairs; the first warning for breakfast. The other girls began filing out of the dormitory. Theresa lingered. She looked at Clara. Not directly—just a flick of her eyes in the mirror. Then she followed the others.

Hidden Seams

That morning, after chapel hour was announced and the others drifted dutifully toward the west hall, Clara turned away. She did not seek permission. She did not leave any word. She simply vanished, slipping through the laundry yard with her satchel hugged to her chest.

She needed to be alone.

Ms. Barstow had encouraged the girls to speak of their dreams after catching some of the gossip. It turned out several girls from other dormitories dreamed of amber or golden treasures speaking to them. Clara alone understood how this was possible but remained quiet while arguments broke out about who was being honest and who was lying about their dreams.

Their French instructor seemed to believe all of them, and Clara felt as if her conviction went deeper than just pacifying the quarreling girls. She began to fear that the stone had reached out to adults as well. Her fears slowly began deepening her guilt and shame for bringing the gemstone into Wetherby Academy.

Her mind ground over why she hadn't handed the stone off to one of her father's lawyers. Or just let the damn thing sink to bottom with…her family. Clara stopped and sucked in a breath. The thought of her lost family blindsided her hard again. She resumed her march along the unkempt and overgrown path that twisted behind the old orchard. It ran past a collapsed well and a heap of broken stone where a sundial had once stood. No one else ever came this way. Maybe the other girls really did believe the place was haunted.

Clara hoped there was something after death. She prayed that the ghosts of her family were in heaven. But in her darker moments she remembered ghosts haunt the place where they died.

The chapel was still in morning shadow when she reached it. Light filtered in through holes in the roof and broke into slants through the tall, eyeless windows. Dust hung in the air like sleep not quite shaken off.

Clara moved effortlessly through the debris. She sat on the same block of cold stone near the altar and opened her satchel. Inside: a folded chemise, her sewing kit, and the thing she had carried since the sea had swallowed her family whole.

She took out the amber gemstone.

It glowed softly even in the filtered light, the face within barely visible—shifting slightly, depending on the angle. Not alive. But not inert, either.

Clara set it down carefully beside her. She unfolded the chemise on her knees, reached for her needle, and began to thread it.

Her fingers trembled a little and it took her several tries.

She glanced up at the rafters.

"I hope you didn't see that," she said, softly, "if you're there."

She bent to her work. The needle pierced the linen cleanly, and she began to stitch a small square of muslin into the inner lining. Tight, even stitches, just as she'd been taught.

"I think it's making them dream," she said. Her voice was steady but hushed. "The other girls. Not just me."

The needle flashed. In, out. In, out.

"They're seeing the gemstone in their dreams too." Clara didn't put a name to who she was speaking to, a ghost, her father, God. She didn't want to analyze her actions; she just wanted to talk to someone. To try and sort it all out. Hopefully she would even come up with a plan to fix it all.

Perhaps she was being naive, but what else did she have to cling to. It felt a bit like being lost at sea, a thought she promptly banished from her mind.

She tied off the corner and rotated the chemise slightly in her lap.

"I am sorry I brought it here and exposed all of them to it."

She wiped fiercely as tears of frustration welled up; she would not cry anymore; it was time to grow up.

"I don't know what it wants. But I know it can't have me, and maybe that is my advantage."

The air in the chapel felt like it thickened, as if listening to her words. Or it was her imagination. Either way, no answers came from the dusty silence.

She folded the last edge of the pocket, slipped the gemstone inside. It nestled there in its hidden place.

She wanted to say more, but all she could see before her was the same path. Her mind was grinding over the same thoughts and observations, and she was developing a headache, high and tight behind her eyes. So, she sat in silence for a time, her eyes closed, forcing her mind to focus on a warm day in the park. It had always made Clara feel better.

It no longer did.

Clara stood with a sigh. She hadn't really thought some answer would emerge from ghostly lips to aid her against the entity in the amber. But she was desperate, and in this situation—in well over her head.

Clara resolved to keep the gemstone hidden. Maybe nice dreams were all it would bring to the other girls.

The thought left a bad taste.

Clara left the chapel, not noticing the shimmering motes of dust that trailed in her wake.

Mabel

Clara stepped over the chapel's threshold, the late morning sun struck her eyes in a flat sheet of light. She blinked. For a moment, the stillness inside still clung to her, mossy and cool, like moisture on skin. Her satchel was tucked firmly beneath one arm; the linen chemise folded neatly within. The hidden weight of the amber gemstone was close enough to thrum against her ribs.

She adjusted her coat and started down the path, skirts brushing through bramble. Then—

"Is she here today?"

Clara spun.

Mabel Finch stood just off the path, her figure slim between two crooked trees, boots in the soft moss, her black stockings, muddied at the ankles. Her spectacles caught the light like twin flashes of fire in a foxglove. She wasn't smiling. But her hands were folded in front of her like she was trying not to look too eager.

Clara's heart hadn't quite slowed. "You startled me."

"Sorry," Mabel said. "I didn't mean to." She stepped forward, not quite meeting Clara's eyes. "I've seen you come here before. I come too, sometimes. I… like the quiet."

"I thought that you didn't believe in ghosts," Clara said.

"Oh, I believe in ghosts, and I believe in their stories," Mabel clarified, "I just don't believe in *their* stories."

Clara took that to mean the other girls in the dorm. She couldn't blame Mabel, some of their stories were just batty.

Clara hesitated. Then: "You believe the old stories?"

Mabel nodded once. "Oh yes. All of them. Especially the wrong ones."

Clara tilted her head. "Wrong ones?"

"Yes, not all of the stories are similar," she explained, "some of the stories place the ghost in the cellars, and still older stories claim that there is an abandoned mine under the school."

"Wow," Clara was impressed. "You know a lot about this ghost."

"You know the chapel's history, don't you?" Mabel asked. "The official version? That it was sealed because it fell into disrepair?"

Clara shrugged. She had not cared where they were sending her and so asked no questions nor read any of the literature provided by her father's lawyers.

"That's not what the older girls say," Mabel continued. Her voice dropped, not for secrecy, but respect. "They say it's haunted. But not just haunted. Cursed. That a girl died here. A long time ago, when the school had just opened. That's when they closed the old chapel and built the new one in the school."

Clara felt the chapel's gaze on her back, even in the open air. "How did she die?"

"That's the part no one agrees on." Mabel stepped closer, voice low and steady. "Some say she took her own life. They say that she locked herself inside and drank something bitter from a chalice on the altar. Others say they found her with a stone in her mouth; her fingers all bent wrong. That's why they boarded it up. So that it wouldn't happen again."

"And the rest?" Clara asked, unable to stop the shiver that brushed her spine.

Mabel looked her in the eye now. Her gaze was too steady for a girl her age.

"They say she was buried alive. That she knew something she shouldn't. So, they dragged her in there, barred the doors, and left her in the dark."

"They?" Clara pressed, but Mabel only shrugged.

Clara swallowed. "That's awful."

"It is," Mabel said softly. "But I don't think it's true. Not entirely. I think she stayed, chose to stay. For a reason."

"And what reason would that be?"

"To watch," Mabel said. "To listen. To wait for someone who'd ask the right questions."

Clara was silent. The path between them filled with the sound of wind nudging through the trees.

"I talk to her," Mabel added, more quietly now. "Not always out loud. Sometimes just... inside my head. She doesn't answer. But I think she listens. I feel her listening."

Clara looked back toward the ruined chapel. The shadowed doorway stood open like a mouth halfway through a word.

"She listens," Clara echoed.

A small silence passed between them, soft as moss.

Then Clara asked, "You don't think she's angry?"

Mabel shook her head. "No. Just lonely. I don't think she wants to frighten us."

Clara nodded slowly. "I think you're right."

They stood like that for a time, shoulder to shoulder, the quiet binding them in ways nothing else at Wetherby had managed. The cold, the rules, the spiteful glances of older girls—all of that seemed thinner out here.

Clara turned slightly. "You can come with me next time. If you want."

Mabel smiled. Small, but real. "I'd like that."

Together, they turned back toward the school. Behind them, the chapel slouched deeper into the hill, quiet and watching.

Inside, in the dust-lit hush, something shifted slightly above the altar—no louder than a sigh.

Just a presence.

The Thing in Amber

The dormitory reminded the entity of the gilded prison it had just escaped.

Rows of narrow beds. A chest at the foot of each one. Shoes lined up perfectly beneath the beds that were being used. Perfect, terrible, order. A prison within a prison.

And what's worse: occupied by children. Muffled snores and whisper-giggles and the unbearable churn of adolescent uncertainty plagued its days now. But still, it was free again. And it intended to make the most of that freedom.

But perhaps not here.

Such places reeked of half-formed identities and scraped-together willpower. They were loud with silence, the kind that spoke of shame not yet ripened, desire not yet named. There were no brash or reckless spirits here. Only children and their world-weary, unimaginative caretakers.

It had spent too long trapped in the Maharajah's treasure horde. Buried beneath heavy coins and elaborate jewelry. Trinkets covered treasure for too long before a German torpedo had burst its prison wide.

Fear of being returned to the Maharajah and his damned baubles kept the entity from reaching out to any the adults that surrounded Clara up until now. But here, the Maharaja could not touch it. It longed for the days when it could move like a breeze, a shadow, a dark thought. Now it moved as a golden trinket.

Now the entity needed to find a suitable possessor.

It considered Mary Barstow. She had fire, and it burned bright. But her heart was too invested in others, it could take years to break her. No, better to find a way out of this academy and back to the cities of man. Back to the banquet it had been denied for *sooo* long.

The gemstone had glutted itself on the young minds since arriving, and while the fare may be lacking in substance, it did give the entity insight to the young humans and their families. And their wealth.

The girls of Dormitory C settled into their beds, their thoughts fluttering like moths just beyond reach. Dreams trickled in like wet ink. Clara's, as always, were thin and grey-edged—salt and darkness, the sound of metal tearing. She dreamt in shapes of loss, not of longing. No fancies to influence and form into a tool. No cracks to pry open.

The entity had grown bored of trying.

It had known, from the moment it was pressed into her flesh that the girl was useless. She was indifferent to its charms. She did not want what it offered. Her soul had come through fire and returned darkened and bleak. She suffered in a self-induced prison of guilt and shame. She saw none of the resplendent sights it showed her. Heard none of the engaging whispers.

But the others…

Yes. The others were more open to the entity's persuasions. It had given Clara one last chance the previous night, and she scorned its offer, again. No more.

Lottie, perhaps, with her clever tongue and the bandaged finger and the wound she kept opening just to watch it bleed. Or the fiery one, Cecily—whose predilections ran far darker than any of her peers or instructors realized. The spirit had tasted something in her once. A flicker. A seed. Not yet germinated.

It needed time. Time and heat.

From the edge of the dormitory, where the frost rimed the windows, something moved.

The entity felt it the way a stone feels weather—pressure, a shift, an added weight.

The ghost again.

It had no name, not that it remembered. No shape worth naming. A relic of regret and unfinished deeds, trailing grief like an anchor.

It was hovering now, just beyond the windowpane above Clara's bed. Watching. Wanting. Wasting its ruin on the only girl who could not be moved.

The entity did not bother to attempt to communicate with the specter. Such things were beneath it. The ghost was made of old scars and lost dreams. There was no vanity in it. No hunger. No fire. Only sadness, soft and cloying as the smell of clay and death.

The entity withdrew inward, curling deeper into itself, and turned its attention back to the room.

One by one, it felt the other girls drift into sleep. It pressed lightly against the edges of their dreams—feather-soft, patient. The entity had learned long ago that corruption was not an act of violence, but of love. It was a friendship. A whisper. The offering of an imagined self: more beautiful, more powerful, more wanted.

Clara rolled in her bed, restless, but the spirit ignored her. It was not her it watched.

Across the room another girl stirred, her face turned toward the window.

And when she did, just briefly, it tasted the edge of something bright and hot—a flash of loneliness, a pang of wanting to be needed.

There; it settled, at last.

The amber jewel

DAY 4 ~ Breakfast, Observed

Morning slunk in under a pewter colored sky that cast the dining hall in a light that was neither warm nor cold, just grey.

The girls filed in two by two, same as always, shoes wet with dew, collars stiff with starch, the heels of their hands still pink from the chill water at the basins. Clara moved quietly along the edge of the procession, her satchel slung tight to her side and slipped into a seat at the long table—far from the hearth, where the favored girls gathered, but not quite so far as to draw a prefect's correction.

A moment later, Mabel Finch appeared beside her, clutching a tray.

"I saved the heel," she whispered, sliding the crust of brown bread onto Clara's plate with a conspirator's flourish. "Best part, if you soak it well."

Clara smiled. "Generous of you."

Mabel shrugged, but there was color in her cheeks.

They ate together in the hush between bells. Steam curled from chipped mugs of barley tea. Around them, the rest of Dormitory C murmured in low voices—some still half-asleep, others already whispering behind their hands.

Mabel leaned close; her voice was low but bright. "I've been thinking about the ghost."

Clara didn't glance up from her bread. "Of course you have."

"I think she wants something from us. Not just attention. Not just prayers." Mabel took a bite, then continued through the crumbs. "I think we could help her. Or free her. Maybe she's waiting for someone to finish the story."

Clara's brow lifted. "What story?"

"Her story," Mabel said. "What happened to her. Why did she die." She hesitated, wiping her fingers on her napkin. "Not just the stories, the truth."

Clara considered that. Mabel was brighter today, more open. Her voice had a lilt to it, like a bird testing new wings. She wasn't folded in on herself like usual, glancing over her shoulder and trying to watch everyone at once.

It suited her.

As Clara watched, Mabel's glasses, clearly too large for the young girl, slid down her nose. This prompted Mabel to push them back into place with a finger. Clara realized that she could draw a direct link to how passionate the blonde girl was at any moment based on the frequency with which she had to push her glasses back on her nose.

Clara took a slow sip of tea and watched Mabel ramble on about names. She believed if they could find the ghost's name, it might loosen whatever had rooted her in the chapel stones. Even setting the spirit free.

"What about the stories about the cellars and the old mine?" Clara asked, "do you think it's the same ghost or a different one?"

Mabel's eyes went wide, and she held her small fists to the sides of her head. "Two ghosts, why didn't I think of that?"

Clara smiled at her friend's drama.

She spoke of archives, of forgotten ledgers, of the old choir plaques in the upper hall.

Clara listened.

She wanted to smile more than she did. But the dull weight under her collarbone never left. The amber was still warm. Still waiting.

Clara had noticed a change in the dining hall. Voices became more hushed, a quiet collective that communicated behind a raised hand, then glanced her way. Some of the girls stared too long, or not at all. Conversations stopped when Clara's attention passed over them, then picked up again after she looked elsewhere. Even Cecily, who never missed a chance to scorn or slander, had grown quiet, her gaze had become sharp and predatory.

Theresa didn't look at Clara directly. She didn't need to. Her presence at the hearth end of the table seemed to pull at the other girls like gravity. When she raised her cup, they raised theirs. When she laughed, low and polished, they laughed too.

She shifted slightly; the hidden weight of the amber tucked in the lining of her chemise.

Mabel was still talking—soft, excited, her eyes shining behind her glasses.

"They always say ghosts linger because something was unfinished."

Clara nodded, though her gaze had turned distant.

She could feel it now—like a storm gathering behind low, gray clouds. That sense of eyes on her. Not just watching but *wanting, calculating, planning.*

This was the work of the gemstone. The amber was manipulating the others. Shaping minds with intent. Increasingly she feared its intentions were dark. And Clara had a bad feeling that those dark intentions involved her.

Clara took another sip of her tea and fixed her expression into something still.

Mabel leaned in with a secret smile. "I think we're meant to find her."

Clara, quiet as the chapel's breath, replied: "We already have."

At the table across from them, a girl with perfect posture and too-still eyes bit into her bread and watched her with an unblinking stare.

Excised

The upper halls of Wetherby were colder than the rest of the school, and quieter.

Their footsteps echoed in the long, high-ceilinged corridor, where the plaster buckled in places and the light from the tall narrow windows struck the floor in long, uneven angles. Dust caught in the beams like smoke. No one came up here anymore, save for the odd prefect tasked with inventory or punishment detail. Even then, not often.

Clara and Mabel walked slowly.

"There are so many," Mabel murmured, brushing a cobweb from the brass plaque affixed to the wall beside her. It read: Choral Class, 1819 – Miss Adelaide Marchmont, Mistress. Below it, a list of names in orderly rows, engraved with pride, but offering nothing more than ink and time.

They had gone through almost a century already, tracing the etched lines with fingers gone cold. The plaques were pious, neat, and thus far, useless.

"Maybe she didn't sing," Clara said.

"Everyone sang," Mabel muttered. "They were forced to. Every girl. Part of chapel."

"But she might've stopped coming," Clara offered gently. "If something happened before her final year. If she was—"

"Buried alive?" Mabel whispered, with a ghost of a grin.

Clara rolled her eyes. "You said that, not me."

They turned from the plaques and made their way down the gallery where the older class portraits hung in neat rows. The earlier years were captured in daguerreotype, all stiff collars and hollow stares, girls caught in a moment they didn't fully understand, their youth pinned to paper like moths.

Farther along, the portraits gave way to drawings: ink and charcoal renderings, stylized and slightly too clean. Dozens of girls in identical uniforms, faces individually sketched, some with lopsided eyes or ghostly expressions. Clara was neither surprised nor disappointed with the results. Mabel's plan, while inspired, contained a number of potential flaws.

They were seeking the name and the likeness of any girl who failed to appear one year to the next. This could work so long as every girl was required to attend chorus, as Mabel believed, and if that girl had not been a senior who graduated and therefore left the school, or so long as she had not arrived after pictures, such as Clara herself had done.

The second issue they encountered was the numbers of girls that *did* meet the criteria. Clara had stopped counting at thirty-seven, driven along by sheer curiosity thereafter. She wasn't overly concerned, if Mabel was right the ledgers would contain more specific facts. Now she just examined the faces of young girls who slept in the bed she now used. Ate tasteless meals in the medieval dining hall below. She wondered what burdens they carried.

She noticed how many girls there were in the school's past. One array of stylized young woman caught her eye. The rows of girls dwarfed the number of students she shared the academy with now. And staff too, she noticed.

Clara stopped and stared closer.

"Look at this," she murmured.

Mabel turned.

The portrait was dated 1807. The year had been carefully penned in calligraphic ink on the faded matting. Ranks of girls stood in a stylized arc around a woman who must have been their headmistress. All wore the same narrow-sleeved gowns, and though their faces were more suggestion than likeness, each had been named beneath in careful script.

Except one.

The bottom-left corner of the drawing was marred—violently. Not age, not wear. Something had scraped it away. The girl who once stood in that space had been obliterated. Not faded, not rubbed out, but erased with intent.

Her outline was gone.

Her name, illegible.

The paper was torn just at the edges, like someone had tried to cut her out and stopped halfway through.

Clara leaned closer.

"There," she said. "Look at the year."

Mabel nodded slowly. "1807."

The air felt colder now.

Clara stepped back; eyes narrowed. "Every girl is named but her. That's not a mistake. That's intentional."

"But why not just blot out her name?" Mabel asked.

"Because someone didn't want her remembered," Clara said. "Someone wanted her gone, as if she never existed."

The damaged space pulsed in her vision, a silence louder than any scream.

Part of Clara was stunned; she had followed the logic behind Mabel's plan, but she never thought it *could* truly succeed. Choosing to pursue Mabel's plan had paid off. Her faith in Mabel was justified.

She turned to Mabel. "You're really smart, Mabel."

The blonde girl smiled and blushed at the rare compliment.

"Tell me again. About the archives."

Mabel hesitated. "They're in the Records Office. Behind the desk, along the wall. All the old registers, all the disciplinary ledgers… they go back centuries. I saw it when we had to carry last year's files up for storage. But it's locked."

"No." Clara corrected. "The sign says 'Keep Door Locked at All Times', but the lock is broken."

"You just tried it?" Mabel asked.

Clara shrugged. "I was in there the day I arrived. I spent some time in the less…crowded areas of the school. That's how I found the old chapel. I saw it out the window in the Records Office."

"Well, we know what to do next."

"We should wait until later," Clara said. "We'll be late for supper if we don't leave now."

The faces of the 1807 class watched them dispassionately as they left.

And one void, scraped into the page marking a forgotten stain.

Escalation

The dormitory was thick with the hush of evening.

The rain had returned, soft and persistent, running in crooked rivulets down the leaded windows. Lamplight flickered in oily pools across the stone floor. Girls moved through their bedtime rituals with the mechanical grace of routine—buttons undone, stockings rolled, hair brushed into obedient braids.

Clara returned to her cot to find her satchel had been opened and its contents scattered across the small bed; a couple of items lay on the floor. Ada, Cecily, Lottie and Maisie were in the room when she arrived, but none of them spoke or even looked in her direction. Clara caught herself before she unconsciously laid a hand on the jewel in its hidden pocket. Time that had not been wasted after all.

She set her bath kit down on the bed and silently collected her items, placing them back in the satchel. Clara sat on her cot, towel around her neck, her fingers damp and red from the chill water in the washroom. She reached for the plain tin box that held her bathing supplies and flipped the lid open with a soft click. Inside, nestled among folded flannel and a cracked comb, lay a bar of soap.

It reminded her, uneasily, of the gemstone. Not in color, but almost. The soap was paler, chalkier—but in the shape. The weight. The way it had been touched. Smoothed down not by time alone, but by hands. Countless hands.

How many had held the amber before her? How many hearts had pressed it close? Prayed to it? Lied for it?

And how many of them had died for it?

She stared down at the bar of soap in her palm and felt the pulse of the gemstone beneath her chemise, snug in its hidden seam.

What had she unleashed on Wetherby?

And why didn't it affect her in the same way as the other girls?

Lost Beneath the Ink

Later that night, after the lamps were extinguished and the fire had settled into a warm mound of orange, two girls stirred.

Clara slid from her bed silently, bare feet making no sound on the cool floor. Mabel rose a moment later, already dressed under her blanket, her spectacles catching the moonlight like a signal. She clutched a small oil lamp to her chest.

They didn't speak. They didn't need to.

Together, they crept down the corridor, past the sleeping dormitories and the darkened chapel hall, then up until the boards creaked beneath their weight and the ceiling arched lower above their heads.

The third floor smelled of dust and wood polish. The banisters here were thick with cobwebs. No girls came here. Few staff. It was too near the attics, too full of things best left forgotten.

They turned left at an old geography classroom and found the door they sought.

The Records Office.

Mabel tested the knob. It turned, just as Clara had promised. They slipped inside.

Mabel lit the lamp. The wick caught with a soft pop, casting flickering gold light across the desk. Shadows clung to the bookshelves and corners.

Clara didn't wait. She moved to the far wall, where the older volumes stood. Ledgers bound in cracked leather; spines labeled in a small, exacting hand.

There.

Admissions, 1800–1825.

She pulled it free with care. The book was heavier than she expected, swollen slightly from age, as if it were bloated from holding too many secrets for too long.

They climbed to the third floor's western stairwell landing, where the window alcove offered just enough space to sit and read. Mabel set the lamp between them. The flame swayed as if nervous.

Clara opened the ledger.

The pages were brittle at the edges but intact. The ink had faded to brown, the lines written in a beautiful, almost musical hand.

They flipped past years. Girls entered. Girls left. Neat notations in the margin; transferred, expelled, married, deceased.

And then—1807.

They stopped.

There were several pages of names for the large class, in fact. And then they found a line that was marred. Not empty. A name had been there, but it had been scribbled out.

Not struck through. Not neatly blacked over. It had been destroyed, ink spread repeatedly across the lines, letters faded into shadow.

But the human hand is imperfect, and time reveals all.

The ink, for all its applied violence, could not entirely obscure the past. Clara knew there would now be no need to compare the names in the ledger with those on the portraits. The attempt to erase the girl had been circumspect.

Clara leaned closer. The name was there—at least the first name—ghostly, like breath on cold glass. She tilted the ledger, bringing the page in question before the lamp's glow, exposing the shadowy remains of a name.

"Mabel," she whispered. "Do you see it?"

Mabel squinted. "Wait. Yes…"

And then, together, they read it.

"Marguerite."

The inky assault had failed to fully erase her. The young girl's name remained, faint but undeniable.

Marguerite.

Clara sat back against the alcove wall. Her breath trembled.

She had a name.

The ghost had a name.

Clara felt a thrill of satisfaction for a job well done. Well, at least the first part. As for freeing a ghost, Clara remained skeptical, and a little concerned about even trying. And to herself alone, she remained divided over whether she wanted the ghost to even exist.

Of course she wanted to see her family again. But if that

Marguerite

meant they had to exist as ghosts, trapped at the bottom of the Mediterranean sea…

But if ghosts were real, and she could free Marguerite, then maybe she could free her family too. One day. That would be something to look forward to.

Something to work for.

To live for.

The more rational part of Clara's mind pointed out the absurdity of her dream, but grains of hope, no matter how small, are tempting treasures to the hopeless.

But why was the girl erased?

Clara ran her finger along the rough, brittle parchment to the column at the far right where the word 'Errant' was still plainly visible.

"Errant?" She questioned.

"It means she ran away from Wetherby," Mabel explained. "If nobody knew what happened to her, then they might think she ran away."

"If nobody knew what happened, then why did they try and remove all trace of her?" Clara pointed out. She ran her finger up and encountered more 'Errant' entries. Sixteen including Marguerite.

Mabel breathed over her shoulder, "what if something bad happened to all of them?"

"Maybe Marguerite can tell us," Clara suggested.

She looked at Mabel, who was staring at the page as though it might crumble if she blinked.

"We'll talk to her tomorrow," Clara said, though she knew neither of them would sleep a wink tonight.

Infection

The fire had burned out hours ago.

Headmistress Ebsworth sat alone in her room, the curtains drawn tight against the rain-slicked dark. No lamp. No candle. Just the mirror before her, reflecting her silhouette in fractured silver.

The dressing table was an old one—polished walnut, the varnish dulled by decades of use. She had brought it with her to Wetherby years ago, though she no longer recalled where it had first belonged. London, perhaps. Or her mother's house.

Now it was a place to forget. A place to let slip from memory all those things she could not control. And the alcohol helped. She took another sip of the foul stuff. She had to admit it worked, she had forgotten why she sat down at the table in the first place.

Eileen was not a drinker, social or casual. She never had been. So, when her ears popped, she attributed it to the weather. The sudden creaking of wood as something manifested around her, and the stillness of the air went unnoticed in her altered state.

The creature's mind entered the room, though it would be more apt to call it a proboscis. Its presence displaced air in the small room that created a brief breeze that disturbed her hair. Confused, Eileen swatted the air as if chasing an insect. It settled over her head despite her actions; it was intangible to the human.

The monster examined the radiant filaments of thought that linked her to the other minds in the academy. But something was wrong. The strands of energy were dull, and many were deteriorating as it observed them. It moved deeper, from surface thoughts into the autonomic system.

Here it found the problem. This human's system was flooded with a toxin.

The creature interrupted Eileen's brain function, specifically her balance system. Her world suddenly flipped, her orientation lost, she slid from her chair in a heap. Her stomach responded to the vertigo by disgorging the light supper and several drinks she had consumed on the floor. And once again, after a secondary wave of nausea swept over her.

She lay on the floor in a cold sweat for several moments. The creature opened the pores on her skin wider, increasing her discomfort. The filaments began to light up.

It was pleased to see many strong connections to one that held the entity; that would expedite matters. It was equally pleased to see that there were no connections between this human and the entity.

The creature had visited the other humans already, leaving their authority figure for last. It was disturbed by how many minds were tied to the entity. If it did not put a stop to the trespasser's feeding, it would soon begin to feel hunger. That was not acceptable.

The monster that lived below the school had discipline, and that kept it on task instead of feeding off the headmistress. Her pain was tempting, but her mind needed to be bent in other ways tonight.

The entity was not inside the young girl, which meant that she was somehow transporting it. The creature also discovered that there were only a few weak filaments between the girl and the entity. This suggested that the girl may not even be aware of the entity's true nature. It knew of several predators that hunted after this fashion.

The Headmistress could simply take it from the child. The creature understood it did not belong to the girl; it had tasted her feelings regarding the entity. The Headmistress would have no sleep tonight. It would take the monster several hours to ensure its dominance over the woman.

After that she would carry out her task: acquire the item that the entity inhabits; then bring it deep into the cave below the academy and cast it into the void of the Deep. This was not done out of any superiority or malice; it was simply the best way to make certain the creature never had to deal with this specific situation ever again.

DAY 5 ~ Name, Restored

The pallid light that escaped the bruised clouds was waning when Clara and Mabel made their way to the chapel. The girls moved quickly across the frost-stiff grass, boots muffled against the old path winding through the tangled hedge and crumbling wall. They did not speak.

A hush had settled over Wetherby's grounds, the kind that came not from peace, but from expectation.

They crossed the threshold of the ruined chapel together.

It greeted them as it always had; slouched in its collapse, windows like hollow eyes, roof caved to the ribs. Dust lingered in the air as if it too had died with the chapel. A bird startled at their approach, launching from a broken rafter with a flutter like rustling parchment.

Clara stepped forward first. Her fingers brushed the edge of the old stone altar. It was cool and pitted, slick with moss in places. Mabel hovered a step behind, stopping to light the small lamp she carried. The silence was thick, and familiar now. But not empty.

They found the remains of a pew that would accommodate them both. They sat and placed their satchels on the ground. Mabel set the little lamp between them and pulled a sheaf of paper and pencil. She insisted that everything they do be documented. For posterity.

When Mabel had everything arranged, she looked at Clara, who gave her a nod.

"Hello, I know I haven't been here in a while," she held her hands up apologetically, "I'm a rotten friend. But remember we talked about finding your name? Well, thanks to Clara we have."

She glanced at Clara again, who encouraged her with another nod.

"We know your name," she said, "at least your first name."

The chapel did not respond.

Mabel explained, her voice soft but clear. "It was scratched out. In the archives. They tried to erase you. We wanted you to know, you haven't been forgotten." She let the silence receive it.

Then she said the name.

"Marguerite."

The air trembled faintly. Just a breath. Just enough to stir the dust near the altar, though neither of the girls noticed.

Clara saw that Mabel's glasses had slipped down again, and upon closer examination she realized the small girl was truly wearing adult-sized spectacles.

"Mabel those glasses are huge."

"Ya," the blonde girl replied sheepishly. "My others are too small, and when I wrote home about needing new ones, these are what they sent me."

"Yes," Clara shook her head, "but you're not an adult, your family knows that."

"Well," Mabel fidgeted with the paper, "it's been a few years since I've been home."

"What," Clara asked sarcastically, "a decade?"

Mabel opened her mouth to answer, then did some math in her head.

"Almost."

Clara was stunned into guilty silence.

"I have my old ones, see?" She dug out a small case and snapped it open. When she looked back up at her friend, she wore glasses that looked like they belonged to a doll.

There was a brief pause before both girls burst out laughing.

Mabel slipped the adult glasses back on.

"Come here," Clara took hold of Mabel's head to get a better view of the glasses.

She located the place where Mabel's ear curved down and carefully bent the earpiece down. She repeated the procedure on the other side. She sat back.

"Okay, try it," she urged.

Mabel moved her head around, but the glasses stayed fixed in place. The blonde girl's smile lit up and she began swinging her head about violently. This proved enough to dislodge the glasses and make her dizzy. Clara caught Mable before she fell off the pew, and they devolved into giggling again.

Neither of the girls noticed one of the dust motes in the rafters light up with a subtle glow. And then another. And more.

When the laughter had subsided, Clara pressed her new friend about her family. She tried not to judge Mabel's parents, but right now that required significant effort.

"Do you have any brothers or sisters?"

"Yes," Mabel began doing math under her breath, "I have five brothers and three sisters."

"Are you the youngest?" It was not a blind guess, many wealthy families with several children boarded the younger siblings.

"Oh, yes, all the rest of them have their own families, and some even have children of their own." Mabel leaned in conspiratorially, "I'm even younger than some of my nephews. Mom says I was a surprise."

"I like surprises," Clara replied with a smile.

She was beginning to sketch the boundaries of Mabel's loneliness. And while it mirrored her own in many ways; the root was so very different. It gave Clara a perspective that she would need time to fully appreciate. In that moment she just felt very sorry for her friend, and a little selfish for some reason.

"Do you think Marguerite will tell us her story?" Clara directed the conversation back to lighter topics.

"I don't know," Mabel looked around the ruined structure, "it might take some time to convince her to talk to us."

Mabel stood suddenly.

"Marguerite," she addressed the ghost, "we need your help; tell us about yourself and we'll tell your story to the world. Oh, and tell us about the other ghost too."

They waited a few more minutes before Clara spoke again.

"We should go; we don't want to be late."

The girls collected their things and departed the ruin. Neither noticed the glowing motes that circled in the dim rafters.

Marguerite began to remember.

Searching

Clara and Mabel made their way along the shadowy corridor that led to Dormitory C. The girls created half-serious schemes to discover the ghost in the cellar, or even the old mines. They even planned where they could acquire ropes and shovels. They enjoyed the exercise more than the goal.

As they neared the dormitory, Ada burst out of the room and ran past them. She didn't even spare them a glance. The girls shared a concerned look.

Clara crept up to the doorway and peeked in, and her heart fell.

Headmistress Ebsworth stood by her bed. Her bag had been dumped out again and searched, though this time the items were neatly stacked beside the luggage. Clara appreciated that.

The other girls stood straight, eyes wide with surprise.

The headmistress noticed them and motioned the girls inside the room.

"Ms. Whitmore," she said, her finger pointed to a spot nearer.

Clara complied, entering the room to stand before the Headmistress.

"Ms. Whitmore," the Headmistress looked severely down her nose at Clara. "I believe you have something that does not belong to you."

It was a statement, not a question.

Clara had not spoken to the Headmistress before now, but

she had seen her. And what she saw now concerned her. The woman's eyes were glassy and red-rimmed. Her skin ashen and drawn.

Ms. Ebsworth didn't look well.

"I don't know what you're talking about," Clara replied.

"It wasn't in these things," she indicated Clara's personal effects on the small bed. She held up a hand and motioned, "your satchel, hand it over. Now."

Knowing full well the woman would not find what she was looking for there, the girl did as she was ordered.

Ms. Ebsworth took the satchel and dumped its contents onto the bed. She rifled through the items for a few moments, not finding what she sought. Her eyes fell on Mabel.

"Mabel Finch," she motioned the little blonde girl closer. "Give me your satchel as well."

Clara stood frozen as the headmistress crouched and unbuckled Mabel's satchel. She hadn't intended for her friend to be caught up in...whatever this was.

Mabel's papers and pencils and the case for her tiny glasses spilled out on top of Clara's things. Again, the Headmistress found nothing of interest.

"There is guilt in you, I sense it," said Ebsworth. "You carry it poorly. You keep to corners. You walk where you shouldn't. You speak too little, and only when pressed."

"I've done nothing wrong," Clara said, her voice tight.

"That remains to be seen."

"She's hiding it," came a sharper voice from across the room. Clara turned. It was Cecily, of course. Her eyes glittered like frost. "She's clever, it's not in the bag."

Ebsworth turned. The dormitory went utterly still.

"I will search your person," she said.

Clara's pulse kicked. The amber lay tucked beneath her blouse, warm against her sternum, sewn tight in the secret pocket of her chemise.

"No," came a new voice from the doorway.

Miss Mary Barstow stepped inside. She brought with her a rush of night air, her cheeks flushed from haste, her curls damp at the edges. She moved into the room like a flame into dry paper.

"Really, Headmistress?" She said, smiling. "A personal search? For what, exactly?"

"I have reports from credible sources that tell me she has taken something," Ebsworth said, voice like stone. "Something that was taken from the Persia."

"From whom?" Barstow asked, genuinely interested.

Ebsworth wavered. Just for a second she seemed to doubt herself. She suddenly looked more worn down.

"That is irrelevant," the Headmistress said. She paused for a moment, then walked to the door. She turned back to Clara, "I will be watching, Ms. Whitmore."

Ms. Barstow looked at Clara. Then back to the headmistress. Her expression remained confused. Clara sympathized.

Ebsworth knows about the gemstone, but how?

Barstow reached for Ebsworth's arm. The touch was feather-light. "Let it go."

Ebsworth stared. Then she left the dormitory.

Clara sat slowly. The amber was warm, steady, eager.

Barstow offered a careful smile. "Goodnight, girls."

She turned and left.

Silence swelled in their wake.

Eileen Ebsworth waited until she entered an abandoned hallway before she leaned heavily against the wall.

What the hell just happened?

She had been so certain that Clara had something that didn't belong to her. Something dangerous. But when she was confronted by Barstow, her memory conjured up a discussion with Eleanor Thornton!

Dear God, was she losing her mind?

Eleanor was an idol, the idol, but she had never had the honor of meeting or even communicating with the great woman. Why would she make that up? How could she make something like that up?

What if—oh, poor Clara.

Eileen stumbled her way back to her room. She needed to get some rest. God willing, she would wake and put all this madness behind her.

Lost, Then Found

The dormitory was dark. Rain tapped softly at the windows, a nervous rhythm. The soft rustle of bedding provided the room with its only occasional disturbance. Most of the girls were already asleep, curled beneath their covers, their breathing syncopated like a distant sea.

But Ada Bello was awake.

She lay on her side, eyes wide, staring across the room at the slow rise and fall of Clara Whitmore's back. Ada had watched her all day.

The way she drifted at the edges of conversations, never needing to speak. The way people fell quiet when she walked past. The way her hand sometimes pressed to her chest when she thought no one was looking.

That hand.

It always hovered in the same place.

Not a pocket.

But beneath the fabric.

She wasn't going to steal anything. Not yet. She only wanted to know for sure it was there. The thing in her dream.

Ada had feared the Headmistress would get her hands on it. The golden light had told her so last night; the Headmistress wanted it for herself. The girl would never allow that. Neither would Ms. Barstow. Nor would many of the girls whose dreams were now alight with life.

She wasn't going to take it. Maybe.

The air in the dormitory suddenly felt thicker. It pulsed gently in her head. Even the sound of the rain on glass receded somewhere distant as the moment consumed her.

Ada rose silently; her feet bare against the cold floorboards. She padded across the room in breath-held stealth until she stood beside Clara's bunk.

Clara lay on her side, one arm tucked beneath her pillow. Her face was soft in sleep, but her brow was faintly furrowed, as though her dreams resisted her rest.

Ada reached down.

Her hand hovered above Clara's chest.

And then she touched her.

Just lightly—fingertips brushing the place where the fabric of Clara's nightdress swelled slightly over a hidden seam. A place carefully stitched by hand.

The moment her skin made contact, a wave of heat surged up her arm—not warmth, but recognition. Like touching something alive and awake and watching her from beneath the surface.

The amber, pressed between cotton and skin, was burning.

Her fingers didn't withdraw.

They pressed more firmly.

And something inside the stone saw her.

It saw her shame, her longing, her need.

And it spoke to her now, as it had in the dream.

You could matter, it breathed—not in words, but in sensation.

You could be seen.

All you must do… is want it.

Ada's breath hitched. Her fingers curled slightly.

She pressed harder.

Clara shifted, still asleep. Her brow twitched. Her lips parted.

Ada withdrew her hand as though burned.

Her heart galloped in her chest. Her mouth was dry.

The spirit had touched her. No—claimed her.

She backed away. Returned to her bed and climbed beneath the covers.

But her hand still burned.

DAY 6 ~ Secrets

The day had dawned as morose and bland as every day at Wetherby, but Clara hadn't noticed this morning. Her dreams had been even more confusing than normal. She was certain it had to do with the events of last evening.

Clara was concerned as well as confused. None of this made sense to the girl. She understood the lure of the amber gemstone, but why had its effect on the Headmistress differed so much from the rest of the people it encountered?

The Headmistress looked more dead than alive last night. Contrasted with Ms. Barstow, who was light and lively as she arrived to stop—wait, why did she stop Ms. Ebsworth?

Were they fighting over the gemstone now? How much worse was this going to get?

"Clara," Mabel said again, "are you alright?"

"I'm sorry Mabel," she looked down at the sheaf of paper her friend was writing on, documenting the second day of letting Marguerite know her name. "What did you ask?"

"Do you think Ms. Ebsworth is okay?"

"I don't know Mabel."

"But you do have something," she didn't look up, and it wasn't a question. "Something from the ship."

After a brief pause Clara nodded. She didn't know what to say yet.

"Is that what's in our dreams?"

"Yes," Clara said, "at least I think so. I don't really know very much about it."

Mabel motioned with her pencil toward the hidden pocket.

"Can I see it?"

Clara covered the hidden stone with her hand out of reflex, her eyes confused.

"Ada found it last night, while you were asleep. I saw her, but she didn't try to take it."

Terrifying as that thought was, it only added confusion to current events.

Clara removed the amber gemstone from its hiding place and presented it to Mabel.

"Ohhh, she's pretty, and I love her crown," Mabel remarked.

"What crown?" Clara pulled the gemstone back and examined the woman in the gem carefully, but she saw no crown.

"I think you're right," Mabel said, "about it being in our dreams. It feels familiar."

"I'm sorry Mabel, I didn't know," Clara apologized.

"Don't be absurd, Clara," she looked at her friend over the rims of her too-large spectacles. "How could you have known any of this would happen?"

Clara forced a weak smile.

"Thanks," Clara said, though in truth, it didn't make her feel much better. "I should have known better. I do know better. I know, deep down, there is something wicked inside the gemstone."

"Why didn't the gemstone try to leave you before now?" Mabel asked, she began recording the facts.

"I don't know," Clara admitted. "Even if it has decided to escape my possession, that doesn't explain Ms. Ebsworth's ghastly appearance."

Mabel stopped writing.

"What do you mean? She wanted the gemstone, right?"

"Yes, but Ms. Barstow interceded," Clara pointed out. "I'm pretty sure she was protecting the gemstone, not me."

"So, they're fighting over it."

Clara expressed her doubt with a frown.

"Maybe," she reasoned, "but Ms. Barstow didn't appear by coincidence; someone warned her what was happening."

Mabel's eyes went wide.

"Ada."

Clara nodded, "she's the only one who left the dormitory. So, either they have teamed up against the others, or they were always on the same team."

Mabel cocked her head to one side as she parsed her friend's words.

Clara chewed her lip. "Have you seen the gemstone affect anyone else the same way it has the Headmistress?"

"No," Mabel admitted, "and she's never looked like that since I've been here."

She went back to scratching words on paper.

"That doesn't make sense," Clara repeated. "Of all the other girls, and Ms. Barstow, it has never made them feel worse. It makes them feel…"

"Better."

Clara looked at her friend, head down, pencil scratching away. She suddenly felt guilty about taking that away from the others. Was she just keeping it away from them out of spite?

Clara dismissed her fears; she knew there was something dark about the gem. Something…predatory.

"So why does it make only one person worse?"

"Maybe she wants to hurt it?" Mabel volunteered.

"How does she even know about it?" Clara mused, "None of the others seem to know that I had it. Or that I found it on the Persia."

Mabel pointed her pencil at Clara, "Ada knows."

"True. But how does she know?"

"It must have told her," Mabel answered.

"And the Headmistress?" Clara asked.

"They do seem to be working at cross purposes," Mabel observed. "Unless she found out some other way. Have you shown it to anyone? Have you told anyone since you found it?"

Clara shook her head. No.

The girls lapsed into silence for a time.

"Maybe it's the other ghost," Mabel suggested. "Not Marguerite, obviously."

"No, not Marguerite," Clara replied slowly. She hadn't thought of the other ghost. Honestly, she had doubted its existence, even considering her faith in Marguerite's ghost. Even considering all the strange twists her life had taken in the last few weeks; Clara had simply felt that two ghost stories being real was too far.

"But what would it want with the gemstone?" She asked, "What use would a ghost have for dreams?"

"I don't know," Mable's curiosity was sparked. "Do ghost's dream? Maybe that's all they do."

The blonde girl turned to the chapel at large and spoke.

"Marguerite, do you dream?"

There was no response.

She turned back to her friend, "I think she's not ready to talk yet."

"I hope she's ready soon," Clara replied, "I think we're going to need all the help we can get. Judging by how it's treating Ms. Ebsworth, I would say it is not a friendly ghost."

"Do you think the ghost is affecting people's dreams like the gemstone has?" Mabel asked, "I haven't noticed anyone else looking like Ms. Ebsworth, but we don't see everyone."

Clara shrugged and shook her head, "I certainly hope not."

She paced the chapel, hugging herself against the chill. The sound of Mabel's pencil rasping against parchment was the only sound in the ruined sanctuary. She ran the same questions over in her mind, realizing it was in vain. They needed more information.

"We can't wait for Marguerite," Clara declared. "We have to find the answers ourselves."

Mabel put her pencil down. "Okay, how do we do that?"

"Well, if the ghost is in the cellars, we can go look for it."

"And if it's in an abandoned mine?" Mabel asked.

"Then we find out if the mine was even real." Clara sat back down. "If a mine, any mine, existed in this area there will be a record of it. It may not be written, but some people will remember the stories."

Mabel nodded along as Clara theorized, adding, "we could ask the cooks; they're the oldest people at the academy. They might know something."

"Good, and we can revisit the records room to check on both possibilities. I spent the better part of my first day exploring Wetherby, of course, the kitchen was too busy for me to wander around in much. It makes sense that the cellar entrance would be there."

"Surely there's a cellar here," Mabel observed, "at least one."

"Agreed. Maybe the cooks will be able to help with that too."

"Maybe it's hidden, to cover up the ghost's story, like Marguerite," Mabel suggested.

Clara nodded slowly, "we can't rule it out, not after what they did to her."

The blonde girl scratched out their plan on paper. Clara felt a little better now having a direction to travel, tasks that could be checked off. Whether they worked out as intended or not, at least she knew what to do next.

Among the shattered remains of the chapel roof, through a wide crack in the wall, the soft glow of the ghost leaked. She watched the two girls make the winding trip back to the academy. Neither girl glanced back to notice. Observing them for the last few days had reminded Marguerite of her former life; more than just the regret of losing it. And Clara was right; they needed help.

The ghost had no idea what the entity in the amber gemstone was, it had certainly never been human, but it had woken *the thing under the hill*. It had drawn the monster's attention by preying on its own cattle. Hunting where it should not.

The creature that lived in the caves had no name that survived, and it had a very long, dark history. Ghosts of people it consumed littered the caves below; many even predated any naming of the land on which they died. Some were not human.

But how could Marguerite help? After all, she had failed. She had challenged the creature to protect the other girls, and it killed her. Quite easily, in fact.

The creature broke her will and bared her soul with such ease the very act itself was demoralizing. The ghost still felt the pain, the spoliation of her mind. The humiliation of being so easily cast aside from her righteous mission. All the other girls she had sworn to protect. How many did it kill in the end?

She had no idea. Not every meal makes a ghost.

She thought she could win, she really had. But in truth she had little understanding of what she faced. An old wives' tale, a children's rhyme, bad dreams, including her own. That constituted her knowledge. The rest had been righteous zeal.

Not enough.

The entity in the gemstone seemed to shield most of the students from the monster, maybe that would be enough. She feared it would not. And the monster had been awakened; it would not go back to its dreamless slumber until it had fed. Truly fed.

It existed on fear and suffering. But it delighted in physically consuming its prey when possible. Just as it had murdered Marguerite so long ago. It had taken her so long to die. The ghost could not let that happen to anyone else.

That thought led Marguerite to another: *what if I didn't fail? Yet?*

What if this was exactly where she needed to be to aid the girls? To ally with them against the monster? Marguerite would do all she could. And she could show them what she knew, what she had seen, how she had died. Arm them with tools and weapons she never had.

She could tell them to smash the mirror. She hadn't understood until too late. None of them had. A common thread among the ghosts in the caves.

She felt the monster uncoil itself below and begin slowly sliding up toward the school.

It would never let them leave now that it had awakened. The girls would have to face the monster whether they wished to or not.

This time the ghost prayed things would end differently.

The Tower Room

Evening turned the low grey clouds into murky purple over Wetherby. The rain had passed sometime in the afternoon, leaving the windows beaded with moisture, like the school itself had been weeping. The air was damp with the scent of coal and cold slate.

Headmistress Ebsworth instructed two prefects from different dormitories.

"Go to Dormitory C, gather up all of Clara Whitmore's items and take them to the tower room."

The Headmistress looked…unwell. Her posture, stiffer than ever, appeared more like death rigor than good habit. Pupils dilated to an uncomfortable size, the sight of which felt like a physical assault to the girls. Her voice was clipped, more than usual, and when she touched them, her grip was firm to the point of pain, and equally unyielding.

While neither girl had anything against Clara, they also had no reason to defend her, and they would not cross the shade of Eileen Ebsworth that towered before them. In fear the two prefects nodded their acquiescence to her orders and fled from her presence.

The creature could not be certain why the woman had failed last time. Her mind may simply have needed more attention. It wasn't going to risk failure again; it would maintain control over her mind this time.

While it was strong, and had deep stores of energy to draw from, it still suffered from the effects of exertion. Direct control over a human was taxing. Animals were much easier to control and required far less resources than anything of higher intelligence. Thus, it had planned for a quick seizure of the item, and confined under lock and key. Then it would allow Eileen to rest for a time, before completing her duties regarding the gemstone.

Eileen wished to go to the dormitory by an alternate route from the one the prefects had taken. The creature examined her intent and allowed her to proceed. As the Headmistress neared the hallway leading to Dormitory C, running footsteps could be heard. She waited until Ada Bello raced around the corner into her waiting grasp.

Clara sat at the edge of her bed, braiding her hair with slow, methodical fingers. Her eyes were grainy from lack of sleep. Her body felt dull, as if she had not slept in days, though she knew better. Nestled under her blouse, the gemstone throbbed faintly.

Then she heard footsteps. Not the usual scuffle of slippers. Not the laughter-laced rustle of girls going and coming from the bath. Two girls that she did not recognize entered and spoke quietly with Theresa. The senior girl shot a look toward Clara. It conveyed pity.

Theresa stepped toward her.

"Clara, these girls are here to collect your things," she explained, "you are being moved to the tower room."

The room grew silent, and the younger girls gasped.

"I thought the tower room was for punishment," Mabel declared,

"Clara hasn't done anything wrong."

There was a commotion at the doorway and Ada shot into the dormitory, propelled ungracefully into the nearest bed. She wheeled about, her eyes burning with rage, jaw set in a grim determination.

Headmistress Ebsworth stepped inside, tall and sharp in her black serge.

All movement in the dormitory stopped.

"The tower room is for *many* things, Ms. Finch," she locked her dilated eyes on Mabel, and the young girl quailed beneath the stare.

All the girls were terrified, the Headmistress looked even more fearsome than usual.

"Clara Whitmore," the headmistress said. She then motioned for the two prefects to continue gathering Clara's things.

Clara stood slowly. She felt, more than saw, Mabel rise behind her.

"You'll come with me."

"What for?" Clara asked, voice level, careful.

Ebsworth lifted a thin folio from beneath her arm. "For review. After a concerning number of reports."

"What reports?" Mabel blurted.

The headmistress didn't look at her. "From girls in this very dormitory. From seniors. From instructors. I have a list of incidents that suggest a troubling pattern."

"No one said anything," Clara said. Her hands clenched the hem of her blouse. "Not to me."

"They didn't have to," said Ebsworth smoothly. "Their observations speak volumes. You walk at night. You are seen near forbidden ground. You speak when no one is near you. You have been watched clutching at yourself, as if suffering some malady or fit."

The girls around her began to shift, guilt blooming across their faces like a bruise. Not one of them met her eyes.

Clara felt the heat begin to rise behind her ears. "I did nothing wrong."

Ebsworth's mouth sharpened. "Ah, the clarion call of the guilty."

Clara's skin burned, both from shame and guilt.

"You will be moved to the tower room. Temporarily. For isolation."

Mabel stepped forward. "You can't—"

"I can," said the headmistress. Her voice didn't rise, but it landed like a door slammed shut. "And I have. Miss Finch, I would suggest caution. Your name appears in several of these entries as well."

Mabel fell back, stung silent.

Clara breathed once, deeply. She straightened. "You're making a mistake."

"No," said Ebsworth. "I am correcting one."

Clara turned. Her eyes found Mabel's for a heartbeat. There was no fear there, only fire.

She didn't fight the hands that guided her away.

The dormitory remained frozen behind her.

As she passed through the corridor and down the main stairs, the dull light from the high windows barely reached the floor. The tower loomed to the north, quiet and unused, its rooms reserved for discipline, solitude, or those too ill to be among the others.

The headmistress led her up the narrow stairs, each step echoing like a clock tick, and Clara felt the weight of the amber pressing harder against her skin.

It was not content. It had been working. Manipulating its new thrall, drawing her closer, deeper into its domination. It had been so close.

But this disruption was not Clara's doing. This was the other. The thing below had made its move. Not through influence, but through authority.

It didn't need to tempt humans. It simply removed them. Separation was power. Clara was being unmoored. Even more so after her recent tragedy. It was preparing her for itself.

Not that the entity particularly cared about Clara, but what would happen to it? There was no doubt the creature had something in mind for the amber gemstone. Something suitably horrible so it could attempt to feed from the entity.

And as the tower door closed behind her, the bolt slid home with a sound like finality.

The entity had one last move it could make. And it took it.

The Long Road

The tower room was cold stone and colder silence. The single window was narrow, half-glazed, and the glass radiated the day's chill into the tiny room. The cot was hard, the blanket rough, the table bolted to the floor. Clara had been left with a jug of water, a crust of bread, and her thoughts—none of which offered comfort.

She sat on the cot, knees drawn to her chest, the amber pressed hot and constant against her skin. It pulsed now with a slow insistence, but one that carried an edge. It wanted her to know of its displeasure. And Clara knew. She had pushed forward believing that the amber gemstone could protect her, or at least itself. That proved a mistake.

She leaned her head back against the wall. The stone was cold enough to make her temples ache.

Then—

A shift.

Not a sound. Not a shadow. Just a tilting of the world.

She opened her eyes and her breath caught in her throat. A web of glimmering motes descended upon her from above.

The air thickened—not with fear, not with pressure—but with memory. Someone else's.

Her eyelids flickered. Then fell.

The darkness was absolute.

She was walking—no, stumbling—through a rough cavern, bare

feet torn, hands trailing along stone walls slick with moisture. The air was warm, but wrong. The sound of her own breath echoed too close.

Ahead—light. A soft, silvery glow rising from the floor like a reflection without a source.

She crept toward it.

The light came from a circle in the stone, no wider than a basin. A mirror but not fashioned with glass. The surface was like frozen quicksilver. It pulsed faintly with each of her heartbeats.

And inside it...?

She longed to reach in, to make contact.

She crouched. Reached out.

The moment her fingers hovered over the mirror, pain flared in her chest—not from injury, but from communion.

Then Clara saw others, lured by the glowing god she had discovered.

The people she fed to its insatiable hunger.

Abandoned in the caves, the crude ladder they had built pulled up.

Never to be seen again.

Then it happened to her. Cast out by her own son. Wandering the caves, drawn by the mirror's argent glow. Crushed by its need. Murdered by her own god.

Darkness returned.

It shifted.

The cavern again—but centuries later.

Walls shored up with roughly cut timber and stone. Primitive carvings marked the lintels. Torches burned in crude sconces.

The mirror remained.

Another victim. This one draped in furs, a priest or king—or both—approached the light. His expression was dazed, reverent. He muttered something. Held a blade. Raised it high—

But not at the mirror.

At himself.

Another shift.

Now the stone was smooth. The chamber was no longer a cavern, but a vault. Carved columns. Floor mosaics. A shrine of sorts. Runes traced the walls—languages dead long before Clara's time.

A woman approached. Robes stained with soil and wax. In her hands a staff crowned with bone.

She stood over the mirror. She knew what it was.

She spoke a name Clara couldn't understand. Then another. Words that slipped from the girl's mind as soon as they entered.

She struck at the mirror with her staff.

Then darkness.

Another time.

A chapel, not Clara's, but very similar. Square flagstones. Broken glass. Light filtered through carved screens above.

And there she was.

Marguerite.

Young. Pale. Dressed not in mourning, but in ceremony. She moved toward the altar with purpose—slow, steady.

Clara felt her thoughts. The determination. The fear.

Marguerite had come to destroy it. She had come alone, believing that if she gave herself to it, she might kill it with the sacrifice.

She pulled aside the altar cloth. Beneath it: the stylized flagstone. A carving like a mouth.

Open. Laughing.

And within it: the mirror.

The same silver eye. Waiting. Endless.

Marguerite knelt.

Clara felt her terror. Her conviction. Her understanding—too late.

She raised a rock over her head.

And then—

Nothing.

Only falling.

Only cold.

Only failure.

Clara gasped.

Her back slammed against the stone wall of the tower. She was herself again, limbs trembling, lungs burning as though she'd run a mile. The trance was gone. The silence had returned.

But the memory remained.

Each vision nested within her mind. One fitting over the other in succession, exposing the message within the dreams. The same choice. The same failure.

She pressed her hand to her chest. The amber burned against her skin.

"Smash the mirror," she whispered, breathless. "That's what they all tried to do."

And they had all failed.

Clara rose, unsteady, the ghost's final moments still echoing behind her eyes. Marguerite had shown her what mattered. The answer wasn't flight. Or hiding. The answer was action. The mirror had to be destroyed.

The rusty bolt on the tower door screamed as it was drawn back.

Catching Fire

The rain had resumed by nightfall, and the air in Dormitory C was heavy, thick with the scent of damp wool and the nervous sweat of too many bodies packed too close. Windows fogged from the dampness. Footsteps soft on the cold wood floor. Voices hushed. Girls from all the dormitories had sneaked out of their beds to gather.

They were arrayed about her now, waiting.

Ada Bello stood near the hearth, her eyes brighter than they had any right to be, casting long shadows in the flickering lamplight. Her hair had come loose from its braid, and she looked like a saint in the wrong sort of painting—feverish, wild, and touched by something that was not of God.

Ada burned with anger at her treatment by the Headmistress. Or not the Headmistress. She had seen the woman's eyes. The jewel in her dreams told her about the thing under the school, but she didn't care. She wasn't afraid of it. It wanted the gemstone too, and Ada would not let that happen. Even if she had to kill to protect it.

"It brought her here," Ada whispered, almost reverently. "You all know it. Clara Whitmore didn't just survive. She was saved."

The room stirred uneasily.

"We've all spoken to it. You know it yearns to be with us."

She turned in a slow circle, her bare feet sticking faintly to the wood.

"She's hiding it. Somewhere. You've all felt it—pulling on you. Drawing you closer."

Cecily Pembroke and the older girls were silent, seated in the corner. They did not speak, but their eyes glittered in the firelight like wolves waiting at the tree line.

"Clara thinks she's better than us, smarter than us" Ada went on, louder now. "She hides it away like a shameful secret, denying us its full glory. Forcing the rest of us to suffer. What makes her worth more than you?" She pointed at one of the young girls, then another, "or you? Why should Clara get to hoard it when we all fell it burn for us?"

A younger girl near the window whimpered and clutched her blanket tighter. Another turned and fled toward the door, nearly tripping over her own hem in her rush to leave. But Ada didn't blink.

"This place is cursed," Ada said, voice trembling with the force of belief. "The rot. The silence. The ghost." Her mouth twisted; teeth bared in something too fervent to be a smile. "She rises above it all, and we are left in the dirt. We deserve what she's stolen. We deserve what she has."

A handful of younger girls had clustered around her now, eyes wide, nodding slowly, numbly. One whispered, "I saw it glow beneath her nightdress." Another added, "She was whispering to the walls."

Behind them, Lottie Dunn stood by the dimming coals of the hearth, her eyes locked on Ada but saying nothing.

"We're not stealing," Ada said, almost gently now. "We're rescuing."

Silence fell. A heavy, waiting silence.

Then the door creaked.

Cecily stood. She did not speak. But the look she gave Ada was approval, cold and calculating. The kind that lets others light the fire first, so she can walk over the ashes later.

That was all Ada needed.

She turned toward the door.

"We're going to the tower," she said. "We're going to free the gemstone."

Some girls fled then, skirts flying, their bare feet slapping down the hallway as they went in search of a teacher, a prefect, anyone with authority.

But not all fled.

A small, tight knot remained; girls too frightened to think, too angry to stop, or simply too desperate to feel included in anything larger than their own sadness.

And Ada led them.

Out into the corridor, up toward the tower.

She burned with purpose. With clarity. With righteous fury.

Once she had the gemstone…they would all see. It had promised—no sworn, it would make the world see Ada.

And it would make the world *fear* Ada.

The Ghost's Map

The bolt scraped home with a drawn-out shriek, its iron teeth sliding into place like the punctuation on a sentence. She didn't turn. Didn't flinch.

Locked in.

And another humiliating search of her items by the prefects.

She sat on the edge of the cot, arms wrapped around her knees, watching the last sliver of grey light bleed through the high tower window. The chill had deepened since morning. Her breath barely misted, but her fingers were numb, and her thoughts had curled inward like paper left too near a flame.

Around her, the small pile of her belongings lay scattered, disheveled—violated.

But of course, they hadn't found the gemstone. Because what they sought was pressed against her ribs, sewn into her blouse. Still hidden. Still hers.

Clara picked up the bar of soap. It was slick with age, golden, worn to a soft, curving shape that almost fit the line of her palm.

It smelled of nothing now.

Just the memory of clean.

She didn't cry. She hadn't cried since her second night here. But something pinched behind her eyes as she turned the bar over once, twice, lost in her thoughts.

Then—another sound.

The bolt. Again.

Clara stiffened and dropped the soap on the bed to keep from ruining it in her grip.

She stood as the door creaked open.

And Mabel Finch slipped inside.

She looked flushed from running. Her spectacles fogged slightly at the corners, her cheeks pink with effort or panic or both. She didn't speak right away, only closed the door gently behind her and leaned against it, chest rising and falling like she'd run from the far end of the school.

"Are you okay?" She whispered. "Did they find the gemstone?"

"No. But I had a vision," Clara said. "From Marguerite."

And she told Mabel everything.

Not just vague half-truths, but all of it. The visions given to her by Marguerite. The lost man in the cave, drawn to the silver light. The priest. The woman with the staff. The shrine. The final, clearest image of the chapel—whole, once— before it rotted into ruin. The mouth-shaped flagstone. The strange mirror that must be destroyed.

"They all tried to shatter it," Clara said, "they all failed. Marguerite… she failed too. But she showed me. So, I could learn from their failures."

Mabel had gone very still.

"And now?" She asked, barely above a whisper.

Clara crossed to the window.

The clouds had thickened into low, heavy masses. The sky churned in quiet warning. And far off, near the lip of the hill, lightning cracked across the horizon.

A heartbeat later, thunder rolled in.

Clara's eyes dropped.

The ruined chapel stood like a broken tooth in the fading light; its jagged frame lit briefly by the sky's fury.

And she saw it.

Not what it was now—but what it had been.

A strange building. Angled differently. Stone walls whole. Roof intact. She could feel it—not as a memory, but recognition. Marguerite had shown Clara the way to the mirror beneath the academy.

The chapel was the gateway; the flagstone carved with an open mouth the way down into the earth.

"I know where it is," Clara said. "The flagstone. The silver mirror." She looked over her shoulder at Mabel. Her voice didn't tremble. "It's beneath the chapel."

"And what will you do?" Mabel asked.

Clara turned fully now. Her eyes were sharp. Clear.

"I'm going to go down there," she said. "And I'm going to smash it."

She touched her chest lightly, where the amber lay hidden.

"They've all tried," Mabel said. "They all failed."

She stepped toward the door. Past Mabel.

"But they weren't me."

Behind her, lightning flashed again.

Fall

They had only just stepped beyond the threshold of the tower room, Clara still breathless from revelation, her hand tightening over the amber beneath her blouse, when it happened.

Mabel seized her from behind.

A gasp, sharp and animal, escaped Clara's throat as fingers clawed at her bodice, at the hidden seam. The fabric strained. A stitch popped. Clara staggered forward, catching herself on the stone wall with a thud that echoed like a drumbeat.

"Mabel—?!" she cried, twisting in her grip, seeing not her friend but a face twisted with desperation, eyes glassy and vacant—no, not vacant. Haunted.

"You can't take it down there," Mabel hissed. Her voice was wrong. Tense. Splintering. "It wants to hurt the gemstone."

Clara grabbed at her wrists, shoving Mabel back, but the struggle had carried them to the curving staircase—an iron-railed balcony that overlooked the cold hall below.

Too old.

Too rusted.

And far too fragile.

Their combined weight slammed into the railing—

It groaned—

Cracked—

Gave.

A sudden lurch, the world tipping sideways.

Clara cried out as she felt the balcony shift beneath her boots.

Now, pull her off the edge, kill her.

Mabel's grip tightened. Her eyes flared—some glimmer of herself returning. What was she thinking? She didn't want to kill Clara. Mabel didn't want to kill anyone, most certainly not her only friend in this world.

The girl realized then how she had been used. She had been so certain that she could understand the entity and help Clara. She would be necessary. She would have a purpose.

She should have known better.

"Clara—" she gasped, "I'm so sorry."

She wasn't pulling anymore.

She was pushing.

With one final heave, Mabel shoved Clara back toward the tower door—just enough.

Clara fell hard against the stone threshold, breath punched from her lungs.

Mabel, still on the edge, bit back a scream and dropped.

Her body struck the lower railing, then tumbled, limbs like a broken doll, to the floor below. The sound was awful in its finality, and the following silence.

Clara stared down from the splintered balcony, her knuckles white on the broken railing. Below, Mabel lay in a crumpled heap, her limbs twisted with terrible stillness. One leg bent wrong. Her chest rose in shallow, rapid gasps.

Clara's mouth moved without sound. Her breath had abandoned her.

"Mabel…" she choked, then louder, "Mabel!"

A groan. Weak, but alive. Relief crashed into her like a wave. Clara turned to run for the stairs—and froze.

"Clara killed Mabel!"

The voice was small, shrill, shaking—but it carried.

Clara spun. A knot of girls stood in the arched entryway; Ada at the front, her face lit with cruel, unnatural certainty. Around her, more girls shifted about her like a pack waiting to be unleashed.

A murmur rippled through them like dry leaves catching fire.

Clara walked backwards toward the doorway. "She fell—she saved me—she—"

But they weren't listening.

Ada raised her hand and pointed at Clara. "Find it. Bring it to me!"

They surged forward.

Clara turned and fled into the tower room, but the door only locked from the outside. It was quickly forced open by sheer numbers.

Hands grasped at her from behind—fingers like claws, mouths shouting over one another in a cacophony of betrayal and fear. They swarmed her—screaming, struggling—stronger than they looked in their nightgowns and bare feet.

They fell back on the bed in a knot. Hands roughly pulling her hair and clothes. Her hand came down on something warm and oval.

"I don't want it!" Clara screamed.

She tore her arm free. Something golden clutched in her fist.

She hurled it with all her strength toward the tall window.

It struck the glass with a shatter that silenced the room.

The girls froze. Their heads turned in unison toward the broken frame, where their prize had vanished into the night.

They rushed past her. Out the door. Down the stairs. Gone.

Clara stood in the wreckage of the moment, her chest heaving, her arms trembling. The wind from the shattered window lashed her cheeks.

Then—a sound behind her.

Mabel.

Clara stumbled back to the landing and down the narrow spiral stairs, her feet slipping on the slick stone, heart thundering. Not far from Mabel's head lay her broken glasses, now bent and twisted like her.

Mabel lay still, lips pale, sweat damp on her brow. "I didn't want to…" she whispered, voice hoarse. "It told me…that you would need me. It would let me control it, so…"

Clara knelt beside her, brushed the hair from her face, swallowed the lump in her throat.

"You'll be alright," she whispered. "I promise. I'll fix it."

"Why did you throw it away?" Mabel's voice was growing weaker.

It took Clara a moment in her current state to understand the question. "Oh, no, I have the gemstone here, that was a bar of soap."

"Oh no Clara," the girl's eyes were panicked, "it's telling them that you tricked them. They are coming back. You must run Clara. Now!"

Her eyes flicked to the floor—wreckage scattered in all directions. And among the twisted pieces of railing and splinters of rotted wood—

A metal rod. Thin, tapered. Black with rust. It must have snapped free from the balcony during the fall.

Clara stared at it for a moment, then reached out and took it. It felt wrong in her hand. Heavy. Cold. But solid. Though never fashioned for violence, it should be sufficient to break the mirror.

With one last glance at Mabel—alive, but broken—Clara rose.

And ran into the dark.

Through the Old Paths

The halls of Wetherby had descended into chaos.

Voices echoed through stone corridors like baying dogs searching for quarry. Boots clapped on staircases. Doors opened and slammed shut with blind insistence. The girls had become something else—panicked, alert, hungry. And the staff, half-caught in confusion and rumor, only added to the chaos.

But Clara moved in silence.

She knew the ways that weren't watched. The old paths, no longer taken due to the lack of funds for upkeep and repair.

In her short time here, Clara had traced the school's byways like a second skin—its side passages and forgotten cloakrooms, the servants' stairs that twisted behind the main halls like old veins. She had learned quickly which windows stayed swollen in the frame, which doors never latched right, which alcoves swallowed a girl whole if she pressed flat enough.

Now, these confused girls were the only thing keeping her from reaching the ruined chapel.

She slipped behind a statue of St. Ursula and vanished into a side corridor long abandoned—mildewed, disused, its walls the yellow-grey of old parchment. Through the cracked pantry, beneath the laundry scaffolds, past the lead-paned window where no light ever came. Her damp skirts caught on splinters and loose stone, but she didn't stop.

The thunder was louder now. Still distant, but it seemed to roll closer after every flash.

At a second floor landing she froze, breath held. Voices drifted up from below, bouncing off the walls in strange angles.

"…search the upper galleries—she won't risk the front…"

"…saw her—I swear, she was headed east…"

Then—

A voice above the rest. Clear. Commanding.

"What the devil do you mean, Clara killed Mabel?"

The Governess.

Clara's breath caught.

The weight of those words rang in her chest like a bell. Not because they weren't true—but because they were, in some small, brutal way. She had brought Mabel into the storm. And maybe she had killed Mabel, but if she didn't stop the thing from below and the entity, that maybe would become a certainty.

Because of her.

Clara turned and pressed on. Her footfalls were a whisper, her hand against the stone wall a lifeline.

She reached the narrow stair that led down to the old music room—long locked, but the door had warped from decades of rain, allowing Clara to work the bolt free with the metal rod.

She ducked inside.

And there—shouts.

From below.

And ahead.

Two parties. Converging.

Nowhere to run.

She backed up, her shoulder striking a cabinet—her breath catching—

Then the temperature shifted.

The hair on her arms rose. The shadows thickened around the edges of the room.

And there she was.

Marguerite.

A web of glowing motes in the dark, floating above the floorboards. A figure woven of shimmering threads finer than a spider's silk. The ghost's face was half-formed, her limbs adrift like seaweed in water.

But her gesture was clear.

Follow.

Clara obeyed.

They moved quickly, the ghost gliding like silk along a forgotten passage that should have been a dead end—but at the far wall, behind a leaning bookcase, the bricks were uneven.

Clara pushed.

It opened.

The air on the other side was wet. Cold. Free.

She slipped out into the night.

The rain hit her skin like a benediction.

The wind caught her clothes. Her boots sank into the soft vegetation of the rear garden. She did not look back.

Above her, thunder broke again—closer now. A rolling growl in the sky's throat.

She ran.

Past the orchard. Past the crooked stones of the outer yard. Her feet splashed through puddles, skirts twisting around her legs.

She kept her hand clenched at her chest, feeling the weight of the amber gemstone, still tucked safely in its hidden pocket. Burning—angry.

The chapel rose into view, black against the clouds, its silhouette highlighted by the glow of lightning strikes deep in the clouds above. Clara didn't hesitate. The ghost had shown her the way.

And now, she would follow it to the end.

In the Mouth

The ruined chapel stood waiting in the storm; its broken ribs silhouetted against the dark churning clouds. Clara didn't pause as she stepped through its ancient threshold, her boots soaked, her hair plastered to her scalp by the relentless rain. The iron rod from the banister was cold in her hand, its rust streaking the skin of her fingers like blood.

Marguerite was already there.

She hovered near the altar, more visible than ever before, threads of silvery light knitting her form together in suggestion rather than shape. She no longer flickered uncertainly. Tonight, she stood still and tall, watching Clara with something that felt like grief made luminous.

Clara nodded. "Show me."

The ghost moved—gliding across the cracked stone floor to the altar, and to the stone on which Clara had sat so many times. Then she remembered the flagstone with the 'O' carved on it. The girl realized that it was not an 'O' carved in the stone, but a mouth. Worn and faded to obscurity by time and climate until it faintly resembled the vowel.

Clara knelt across from the ghost. Her palms scraped stone as she brushed the dirt away, revealing the faint edges of a rectangular slab, broader than the others. She wedged the iron rod beneath it and heaved.

Nothing.

She repositioned herself. Braced her foot against the wall and pushed with all her might.

The stone gave a groan like something waking from an old dream.

It shifted.

Again, she shoved—this time with both legs straining with every ounce of strength she could muster. The slab scraped aside, grinding its ancient protest into the chapel floor, revealing a black void beneath.

A stair.

The mouth had opened, and Clara felt an immediate pull, as if the caves below were inhaling after a long spell without breath. A chill rose from the darkness, something more sinister than weather.

Clara hesitated, in her headlong dash she had failed to grab a lamp or candle, not even matches. Marguerite moved closer, urging her on and providing light at the same time. Clara descended, the rod held in one hand, her free hand trailing the damp stone of the stairwell. Behind her, Marguerite followed, glowing fiercely to keep the darkness from becoming absolute and swallowing Clara whole.

The stone tunnel wound downward, spiraling deeper with each step. No torches. No sconces. Only the ghost, and the hush of time pressing close around her ears. The walls began to change. Rough stone became worked stone—etched with crude patterns, worn almost smooth by centuries of passage.

As they passed deeper, Clara began to recognize the shapes.

She had seen them—in the visions. The carved lintels, the split archway, the three-eyed figure etched along the curve of the wall. In the flickering, colorless light of the ghost, the carvings seemed to shift, turning their heads as she passed. Some tilted upward. Others bowed low. Their expressions were lost to erosion, but not their intent.

Some of the figures seemed to twist inward on themselves in a fashion that made Clara feel fuzzy, then the ghost positioned herself between the girl and the wall. The moment passed. Clara began walking again but ceased her examinations of the tunnel's walls.

Then Marguerite stopped.

They stood before a long, narrowing corridor that bent downward with unnatural precision.

The ghost lifted a hand—not to beckon, but to halt.

Clara turned toward her, heart pounding. "You're not coming?"

Marguerite said nothing, only glowed impassively.

Clara felt the cold beginning to creep in—not from the air, but from within herself. She had no lamp. No torch. No matches.

Clara transferred the iron rod to her left hand and retrieved the amber gemstone from its secret place. Its soft, golden glow spilled over the stone.

But then—light. As the ghost withdrew the girl could see it leaking from somewhere down the corridor. Faint, at first. Silvery. Not like Marguerite's glow, soft and sorrowful. This was sharp. Pale and precise. Cold.

It bled from the tunnel ahead, washing the stone in pale gleam. Shadows twisted along the edges resembling sharp, twisted teeth. It was light, but it was a hateful light.

Clara turned back to the ghost.

Marguerite simply inclined her head once.

The last goodbye.

Then she faded, thread by thread, until even her outline was memory.

Clara was alone.

She turned back to the path and stepped forward.

The light drew her in like a current, remorseless and inexorable.

The tunnel sloped downward more steeply now, the stonework tighter, cleaner, but still strange, as if it were built by the hands of people that history had never known. The air tasted of metal and dust. Every footstep felt louder than the last.

Then, rounding the last corner—

She saw it.

A vast chamber, circular and finished, illuminated by that same argent glow. The floor was smooth, rimmed by low stone benches. Symbols curled up the walls like arcane vines. And at the center, sunk into the stone floor like a basin—The mirror.

Waiting.

The Mirror

Clara stepped forward into the heart of the chamber, the light sharpening the deeper she moved. It cut the edges of her shadow into strange, spiraling shapes across the carved floor. The walls, slick with condensation and lined with forgotten faces, seemed to lean closer, as though curious to see what she would do.

Her grip tightened on the familiar warmth, heavy and honey-colored, its smooth surface thrumming faintly. She held it tight, clutching it like a relic, as though its light alone might steady her steps.

It didn't.

Still, she pressed on, breath shallow, boots ringing against stone that vibrated as if it were a living thing. At the chamber's center, nestled in a circular hollow like an eye gazing straight up from the bones of the earth, the mirror waited.

Not glass.

Not water.

Something else.

Silver and glowing, as if lighted from within. Shimmering faintly, as though it responded not to sound or touch, but her proximity.

It was larger than she expected. The size of a proper washbasin, the kind her mother might have once used to bathe her in when she was a child. Not the cheap tin bowls the girls were forced to share, but something solid. Heavy. Purposeful. It hummed faintly, like a murmured conversation just out of reach.

As Clara approached it, something changed.

The warmth in her palm flickered. Then faded.

The amber gemstone went still. Not inert—but paralyzed.

Then the light in the chamber shifted.

Everything inside her opened.

A slow peel, like a wound newly dressed being exposed to air. Her breath hitched. Her thoughts were no longer hers—they unraveled, laid bare to something immense and impossibly close.

It did not speak.

It showed.

The smell hit her first: fire and oil and blood-thick saltwater. Then sound—an explosion of metal, voices shrieking in every tongue, the world tilting with cruel precision. And she was there again, twelve years old and already drowning, her fingers slipping on the splintered rail, lungs seared by smoke.

The Persia.

The shadows above were replaced with flames.

Her mother's hand was gone.

The man's mouth moving, blood in his teeth, as he shoved the stone into her blouse, vanished into the crush.

Not bravery.

Not destiny.

Just damage.

She had survived not because she was strong, but because she had already broken clean through. There had been nothing left for the amber to tempt.

And now, so close to the thing that fed on fear and shame, the stone could no longer protect her.

She fell to her knees.

Tears sprang hot to her eyes, her shoulders trembling as the pressure mounted—*you are nothing, you were always nothing*—a whisper that came from nowhere and everywhere, that lived in her bones. Her body curled, her grip on the gemstone loosening.

This is your truth.

You were never brave. You were hollow.

You didn't resist the amber.

You simply weren't worth the fight.

The amber fought back. Then—it screamed.

A shriek so high and raw that it set her teeth on edge, a burst of searing pain that ran down her arm like electricity through old wires.

It burned in her hand, blistering her palm.

And then came rage—not hers, not human. The gemstone flared in her grasp, turning from warm to white-hot, desperate and furious. It had played her. It had waited. It had tried charm, dream, and temptation. But now, cornered, it turned on her with all the fury of a god betrayed.

For the first time she spoke to the entity. She laughed at the entity. Her grief and her shame had brought her walls low, and exhaustion had taken her fear. Between the two monsters Clara's mind was crushed, leaving only the hardest bits remaining.

Clara acted from instinct, and with a wordless cry, she threw her tormentor at the mirror.

The gemstone flew across the chamber like a streak of burning honey—spun once in the air—and struck the mirror dead center.

The sound was not the shattering she had expected. It was a wet plop.

Then the light winked out like a snuffed candle, leaving Clara in darkness.

Black and absolute.

The Thing Under the Hill

It did not understand.

Not at first.

The silver surface—its sensory organ, its feeding place—had endured for millennia, drawing forth human shame like nectar from crushed fruit. Every victim had come close with the same flickering will: to kneel, to stare, or to strike. All of them ended the same. Dominated. Consumed.

But this…this was new.

The thing hurled into the mirror was not just anger, not just hate. It was inhabited. The amber gemstone entered not as a weapon, but as an invader.

Inside it, something lived, something writhed in fury, spitting invectives. Something that whispered and screamed. Something that lied and begged. Something that cajoled and mocked the fearless ancient from within its own mind.

The creature recoiled. Not because it was wounded, but because for the first time in its long, boundless existence, it was startled.

It tried to withdraw. To pull back.

But there was no way back.

It was in the stone. The Earth. The foundation beneath the mountain of shame and grief that it had gorged on for epochs had left it corpulent. And trapped. In time, as its food supply decreased, its size would likewise diminish allowing it to move to more favorable hunting grounds. But at that moment, it was still bound by earth.

It had been eons since it had physically moved. It had no reference for 'retreat' in its lexicon. Yet some primitive corner of its ancient mind—a mind that predated language, humanity, even this cave—insisted it must get away.

That this thing was *wrong*.

That the whispering stone now nestled inside its eye was not prey.

It was something else.

A thing that caused discomfort. Something that hurt it, and it wouldn't stop.

The entity twisted. It heaved, but its form was vast—its upper half embedded deep into the sediment of time, swaddled in collapsed shrines and ruined catacombs. It had grown vast over the countless thousands of years that it had been fed by cults, explorers, the desperate and broken. Its body had ballooned into a swollen labyrinth of flesh. It *was* the foundation.

And now the foundation buckled.

Beneath it, the Earth groaned.

Vaulted caverns folded like paper. Centuries of hollowed-out worship collapsed inward. Old chambers, forgotten altars, burial galleries—all gone in a single heaving tremor.

Its tails flailed. The superfluous ribs of cartilage crowning the tip of each tail hummed in the air as they flailed, like swarms of angry bees. The long whips thrashed wildly in the dark, lashing the stone with maddened fury. One struck a load-bearing column and shattered it like brittle chalk. Another tail coiled around a stalactite and ripped, sending a shower of stone daggers raining down on its own back.

The entity shrieked—the sounds of collapsing earth buried those cries as surely as its flesh.

It slid.

Beneath it, the floor of the deep fissure crumbled.

Its mass, long lodged in the crust of the Earth, found no anchor.

It fell.

Down into a pit it had once used for excretion. A forgotten abyss so deep even the worms that worshiped it had stopped crawling down.

It fell, and as it did, the ground swallowed itself. A vast sinkhole tore open in a single inhalation. The ground rippled like a stone cast into a pond.

Above, the old bones of Wetherby Girls' Academy groaned in protest, then shrieked in mortal fear. Foundations cracked like eggshells. Stone walls tilted, timber frames snapped. The east wing sagged as though bowing in apology before plummeting into the dark.

The land sank.

With it, the last remnants of those baleful cults, lifetimes of work undone in seconds.

The monster—apex, absolute, eternal—was gone.

Rising

Clara lay in darkness.

Not shadow. Not night.

Darkness.

The kind that pressed against her eyes with weight and meaning, like a great velvet curtain sewn from the deepest of night. There was no up, or down, no sense of the chamber anymore, only the stillness after something unimaginable.

And then, it began. The earth moved.

A soundless warning first—a strange tautness in the air—and then a heaving groan from the walls themselves. A tremor that did not echo but radiated like a shock wave. The floor buckled beneath her, sudden and lurching. Cracks snapped through the stone like whips. Dust bloomed in choking waves.

Clara scrambled backward, slamming against what she thought was a wall. The iron rod clattered from her hand. Stones fell like dry rain. Somewhere, distantly, something massive tore itself apart.

And then she understood.

She had survived the SS Persia. She had lived through fire and oil and the screeches of the dying. But that death—the sea death—had been full of light. Sky above. Screams around her. Something to grasp.

This?

This was dying unwitnessed.

Unremembered.

The sob that escaped her was a dry, broken thing. Her lungs burned from the dust. She pressed her hands to her face, trying not to cry, but the tears came anyway—tears she hadn't shed even when they hauled her, gasping, from the oil-laden water.

But the shock was different this time. It did not dull her senses or mute the noise and confusion. This shock laid her bare, revealed to her the futility of her place. And left her with dark thoughts: would she be lost forever?

Would she too be marked down as 'errant'?

"I'm sorry," she whispered into the dark. "Mama… Papa… I'm sorry. I did what I could."

And then a thought struck her like a hammer: Mabel.

If Clara died here, no one would help her. No one would even know. She pictured her friend lying broken and alone beneath the stairs as the rest of the school tore themselves apart searching for treasure.

"No," she said, voice hoarse. "No—please."

Then—a glow.

Dim. Distant. The faintest point of light, like a star caught behind gauze.

Dust swirled around it, turning the glow into a slow, radiant halo.

Clara coughed violently and blinked away tears. For a terrible moment she wondered if it was the mirror—that it had survived, that it was calling her back to finish what it had started.

This light was soft. Pale as moonlight. It shifted, glided. Not ahead of her.

Above her.

The ghost, Marguerite.

But not in the place she had expected—not in the chamber, not even from the direction she had entered.

Had Clara been turned around?

Or had the world shifted beneath her feet?

She didn't question. She only followed.

Her knees scraped raw on the broken floor as she pushed toward the light. The air thinned as the dust choked her, but the ghost waited. Drifted. Summoned.

The stone around them changed as they moved. The floor no longer bore carvings or chisel marks—just the raw, unhewn skin of the earth. This was not part of the entity's temple. This was something older, more natural. A fissure opened, barely wide enough to crawl through.

Clara slid on her belly, one arm forward, dragging herself after the only thing she trusted in the world. The walls were pressed close on either side. Her ribs ached. Her breath rasped.

But the ghost glowed ahead, never faltering.

They climbed. Twisted. Squeezed through rock that should not have had room for a girl to pass. She scraped her shoulder bloody. Bruised her hip. At one point she sobbed into the stone, gasping for air—

And then—wind.

Cool, smelling of green things. And the scent of rain.

She pushed through a final crack and fell.

Out.

Into the forest.

Clara tumbled down a mossy incline and came to rest flat on her back among tangled roots and ferns. She coughed, hacking dust from her lungs, her body shaking with exhaustion and disbelief and now cold from the winter evening.

Above her, trees reached toward the stars.

The sky was clearing.

The storm had passed.

And hovering overhead, framed against the sky like a dream half-held, was Marguerite.

The ghost hovered in silence, her form clearer than it had ever been—no longer tattered light and memory, but a young woman of quiet strength. Her eyes met Clara's. She smiled—not with sorrow, not with sadness. With peace.

And then, slowly, like morning mist pulled by the sun, Marguerite began to rise.

Her body dissolved into threads of silver and ash, unraveling upward, higher, higher—

Until there was only the sky, and she lay alone.

Clara closed her eyes and wept.

Stop and Listen

Clara thought the trees had never looked so alive. Their leaves glistened wet with storm, each limb trembling slightly in the wind as though still waking from a shared nightmare. The earth under Clara's feet was sodden and slick, but she ran without hesitation—branches whipping against her shoulders, ferns clawing at her already shredded skirts.

Behind her, the place she had come from, that deep and ruined mouth of the world, was sealed again. No light, no sound. Only cold silence beneath the rock. The creature was gone.

But Mabel—

Clara's breath caught as her thoughts surged forward.

She scrambled down the embankment, out of the woods, and into the clearing beyond.

Wetherby was collapsing.

The school shuddered like a wounded creature, large sections of the east wing had already vanished beneath the earth, the land itself torn open along jagged seams. Roof beams jutted out like broken bones, and stone plummeted in chunks into the deepening maw. Tearing sounds echoed from the remaining halls as the wood and stone gave way under stress. Smoke poured from shattered chimneys and from the ground itself.

Clara's heart thudded as she saw girls scattered across the lawns, adults shouting orders with trembling voices. The air tasted of dust and ash.

Where was Mabel?

She sprinted forward, chest heaving, her boots pounding through puddles and cracked slate.

Then—a figure. A dark coat. The headmistress.

Clara barely had time to recognize her before strong hands seized her shoulders.

"Let me go!" Clara shouted, struggling. "I have to—Mabel is still—"

"Clara!"

The voice cracked like a whip. The girl froze mid-step, her breath caught halfway. Eileen's grip tightened. Her eyes, sharp and clear, cut into Clara's.

"Stop and listen, for once," she said, low and fierce. "We have Mabel. Come with me now."

The words struck like a blow to her chest.

Clara went still.

We *have* Mabel.

Not *had*.

Not *lost*.

Have.

"Dear Lord, girl," the woman examined Clara's state, "under all of that dust, I took you for a phantom."

Her resistance drained away all at once. Her knees nearly buckled with the weight of it.

She allowed herself to be turned, to be led. For the first time in weeks, perhaps in her whole life, she didn't forge ahead. She didn't speak. She listened.

And the words lingered, quiet and echoing:

Stop and listen, for once.

She realized how many others had tried to help her—Mabel, always there, willing to sacrifice her own life for Clara. Marguerite, long dead but never still. Even Miss Barstow; twisted though she'd been. And now, even the headmistress.

Before that, her father's lawyers, the secretary who packed her a snack, the old man that met her at the station. How many people who meant well had she misjudged or ignored out of her misguided anger and pain?

Clara pressed a hand to her chest—not to the amber, which was gone—but to the place where it had burned. Something new burned in its place.

Clara turned her head, just once, to look over her shoulder.

The east wing crumbled with a moan of stone and dust. The sky overhead broke open in patches, the clouds drawing away like smoke from a battlefield and exposing it to pale moonlight.

She followed the headmistress, silent and wide-eyed, away from the wreckage—

—toward everything that was left.

All the Quiet Things

The hospital was quiet in the way Clara had come to respect—not silent, not sterile, but quiet with permission. A whitewashed stillness that made space for the business of mending.

Rows of iron beds lined either wall of the great vaulted room, most of them empty now. A few girls dozed or stared dreamily out the high windows. Nurses passed with soft shoes and softer voices. Sunlight flooded the room in broad, golden beams that made the linen sheets glow and the polished brass gleam like melted honey.

Clara sat by one of the occupied beds, arms folded neatly, ankles crossed. She wore new clothes and clean cuffs. Her hair had been combed.

And in the bed beside her, wrapped in splints and gauze and dreams, lay Mabel Finch.

Both of her arms were in casts, one leg pinned and wrapped and suspended from a frame. Her face was swollen with bruising that painted her skin in purples and fading greens. Beneath the bandages, her eyes were shadowed, her cheekbones sharp.

But she *lived*.

The nurses said she would recover—eventually. And Clara had seen enough injuries in her young life to recognize that eventually was a hard-won promise. But it was a promise, nonetheless.

That was more than she'd dared to hope for on the night the tower crumbled.

Mabel had slipped in and out of consciousness in the days since Clara's return from the ruins. She'd opened her eyes long enough to murmur hello, to smile, to try forming the beginning of a joke before sleep had overtaken her again.

The doctors had said Mabel hadn't received any visitors. Her family had wired to say a cousin would look in on her—but days had passed, and no cousin came. And now it was known that Mabel would not be going home. She was being sent on, quietly, to another girls' academy in the northern counties. No note. No flowers. No mother's hand on her wrist.

Clara's gaze shifted to the window where the sunlight poured in. The sky was so blue—bluer than she'd remembered. Mediterranean blue, without the fear. For the first time since the Persia sank, the sun felt like something forgiving. Like a friend. She closed her eyes and let it warm her lashes.

In her lap, she turned the new pair of glasses over in her hands. The frames caught the light and spun it along the curves of the lenses. They were neat, well-made. Chosen carefully. The memory of the old pair—smashed on stone—rose to her throat like a burning thing.

She had them made as soon as she was able to contact her family's lawyers and request new clothes and items.

A small stir beside her.

Mabel blinked against the sun and squinted, her mouth a pale slash in her bruised face. When her swollen eyes found Clara sitting there, she blinked again.

"You're still here?"

Clara smiled gently. "Where else would I be?"

Mabel's gaze drifted to Clara's hands. "You found my glasses."

"They're not your glasses," Clara said softly. "But they are for you. The others were…beyond saving."

Mabel frowned as though searching for memories that still floated just out of reach. "You threw the—thing. Didn't you?"

Clara looked away. "Another time."

Mabel nodded, too tired to press. "It hurts," she said after a pause.

"I know."

"I thought I'd be going home. That's what they told me."

Clara took her hand. Gently, lightly.

"I'm sorry," she said. "But you won't be going back there. You'll be going somewhere else. Another school."

Mabel's lips trembled. "Alone?"

"No."

Clara reached into her coat pocket, retrieving the folded letter with the seal of her father's solicitors. "I'll be going there too. It's all arranged. I made sure of it."

Mabel stared at her, as though the pain couldn't quite keep her from surprise. "You…you are?"

Clara smiled. "Fate's a funny thing."

Mabel's face twitched with the beginning of a smile. Then she sagged back against the pillows, the relief too much to carry with her eyes open. Sleep reclaimed her quickly and Clara sat still beside Mabel, watching the shallow rise and fall of her friend's chest.

Then, slowly, she reached into the satchel at her side and pulled out a thick, leather-bound journal. The cover was rich brown, mottled at the edges, embossed with no name. A pencil was tucked into the spine.

Her mother had always encouraged her to keep diaries. There were boxes of them—half-full, forgotten. She had never liked the look of them. Too small, too neat.

But this journal felt different. It felt earned.

She opened it. The pages were thick, unlined, waiting.

She stared at the blankness for a long time, the pencil hovering just above the surface.

Then, without preamble, she wrote:

They fed on all the quiet things…

End.

Barry

Inspired by STORYFORGE: Advanced Horror Writing Prompts BOOK ONE

PROMPT OPTION 1:

Barry was stunned when the pile of refuse in the abandoned asylum moved suddenly, then raised up to tower over him.

BARRY

From the Podcast:
I Faced Certain Death; and Lived to Tell the Tale
Episode #244
Episode Title: "Face-off"

[PODCAST THEME: low synth drones, cassette tape clicks, reversed whispering voices]

ANNOUNCER *(cheerful, distorted):*

"You're listening to *I Faced Certain Death; and Lived to Tell the Tale!* Where death knocks politely… and our guests slam the door in its face."

LUCA *(loud, cocky, fast-talking)*:
"Good evening, believers, skeptics, and beautiful anomalies from all over the listening world! You're back with your favorite midnight mischief-makers—I Faced Certain Death; and Lived to Tell the Tale!"

"I'm Luca—your host, provocateur, and part-time monster bait."

"And behind that double-thick plexiglass wall, drooling quietly into his third enrichment muffin, is the myth, the legend, the beast—Sassy the Sasquatch!"

(Soundboard click: a gorilla grunt, followed by hollow glass tapping and a long, echoey sigh.)

LUCA:
"He's not much of a talker but trust me—he's got opinions. Mostly about lumber and righteous vengeance."

"But tonight, folks, we've got something special. One of the real ones."

"A card-carrying member of **PEEPS**—that's ***Paranormal Exploration, Examination and Probing Squad*** for those of you who don't spend your weekends hiding in abandoned psych wards with a Geiger counter."

(Soundboard: a warped theremin swell, followed by insect-like chittering and a deep, reverberant thud.)

LUCA:
"His name is Barry. His story is real. And as most of you already know, he's quite a famous chap at the moment."

"Why? You may ask, well I'll tell you. My friend Barry is the subject of the most downloaded image in history. That's right, you know the one I mean. And if you don't...where the hell have you been the last few weeks?"

"Now, for our audio-only crowd, or if you live under a rock, a link to this photo can be found in the episode description."

(Beat. Soundboard: a single, slowed-down camera shutter. Then silence.)

LUCA:
"Barry, welcome to the podcast, the only podcast you have to face death to be a guest on."

(Long pause. A chair shifts as Barry leans toward the mic. His voice is low, deliberate, the voice of someone who's seen too much and talks too little.)

BARRY:
"Thanks, Luca. It's good to be on your show."

LUCA:
"You know, when I was growing up, I had a couple of uncles that worked in the backrooms and I used to visit them at work when I would spend the summers in the city. So, I know how creepy those places can be, but to run into…well, we'll get to that."

"First, let's learn a bit about you and your partner, Marc. How long have you guys been hunting the paranormal?"

BARRY *(does some calculating under his breath)*:
"Two years next month. No, in two months."

MARC *(bumps his mic as he leans in)*:
"Ya, two years in two months."

(Muffled grunting emanates from behind Luca.)

LUCA:
"Don't mind him, he's just laughing at you lifers. What inspired you two to start?"

BARRY *(laughs nervously)*:
"Movies, for me."

LUCA:
"That was all it took? Watching other people get the shit scared out of them? You thought 'that sounds like a great idea'?"

BARRY *(laughs nervously again):*
"Ya, well, as much as I wanted to find a ghost or cryptid, I never really thought about what I'd do if I ever ran into one."

LUCA:
"That's what you get by being influenced by media. How about you, Marc?"

MARC *(bumps his mic as he leans in):*
"So, when I was young, I went on a camping trip with my troop."

LUCA:
"Whoa! Whoa! Whoa! We can't air that stuff."

(Excited grunting from behind Luca.)

"No, everything is not about you, Sassy."

MARC:
"We just encountered Dusk Keepers."

LUCA:
"Oh, that sounds interesting; go on."

(Sassy grunted his agreement from behind Luca.)

MARC:
"So, for hundreds of years hikers in the mountains have reported strange figures watching them."

LUCA:
"And these 'figures' are called Dusk Keepers?"

MARC:
"Well, they have several names..."

BARRY:
"The Watchers in the Night, hill phantoms, mountain shadow people."

MARC:
"Ya."

LUCA:
"So, dusk, night, shadows; am I sensing a pattern here?"

MARC:
"Ya, reports of sightings during the day are rare, but around nightfall they seem to pick up."

LUCA:
"Is that when you saw your Dusk Keepers?"

MARC:
"Ya. Some of the others said they noticed shadows or flashes of movement out of the corner of their eye throughout the day, but the ones I saw were at dusk."

LUCA:
"You saw more than one? How many?"

MARC:
"Ya. I'm not actually sure how many I saw. They appeared every evening on the ridges of nearby hilltops, always with the sun at their back, so all I could see was the dark silhouette of a figure. Or several, actually."

LUCA:
"Did you do any investigating, maybe hike over and see if you could find them or any trace of them?"

MARC:
"No. It might have looked nearby, the ridge where they were standing, but in the wilderness that's a rough hike. Not something our leaders were keen on trying."

LUCA:
"That makes sense."

"So, Barry, movies, books? Anything specific?"

BARRY:
"Um, cryptids, mostly."

LUCA:
"Monster movies, huh?"

BARRY *(laughs nervously):*
"Um, ya, I guess."

LUCA:
"Still feel that way?"

BARRY:
"Um…yes, more than ever."

LUCA:
"Good for you, Barry. Now let me see…"

(Rustle of papers.)

"So, you guys formed **PEEPS** over two years ago. Was that your first foray into ghost hunting?"

BARRY:
"Well, I was a member of Spook Scouts…"

LUCA:
"I've heard of them."

BARRY:
"Marc was already a member when I joined."

MARC:
"Ya, I had been there for…maybe a couple of months before Barry joined. Before that I was a member of another group, but we never really had a name."

LUCA:
"You didn't have a name?"

MARC *(bumps his mic as he leans in):*
"Well, we meant to, but our team broke up fast. Before we had a chance to vote."

BARRY:
"Then Marc and I met in the Scouts."

LUCA:
"And what brought **PEEPS** to the abandoned location where you caught this amazing moment?"

BARRY:
"Uh, the forums."

LUCA:
"The forums?"

BARRY:
"Oh ya, the town is famous, you know, for being abandoned, especially among the paranormal community."

MARC *(bumps his mic as he leans in):*
"And its haunted."

LUCA:
"Got it."

"Now, let me see…you described this as a fully manifested visitation?"

BARRY and MARC (speaking simultaneously):
"Yes."

LUCA:
"And what exactly is that? How does this differ from other sightings that you've experienced?"

BARRY:
"Well, evidence we capture can range from personal observation; something is watching me or someone noticing a moving figure or shadow."

"Witness sightings can include objects moving on their own or disappearing and reappearing somewhere else."

LUCA:
"Do you see a lot of cases where stuff disappears then reappears?"

BARRY:
"I haven't, but the Scouts had several records of that event."

(Barry's chair creaks as he leans forward.)

"The most popular story, which did make the evening news in our hometown, was the *Ebberniche House.* It was a popular haunted house where a lot of us investigators from that area cut our teeth."

MARC:
"Ya, it's actually amazing that Barry and I didn't meet there."

BARRY *(laughs):*
"I hadn't thought of that, but it's true. Anyway, one night a group goes ghost hunting, but the house is gone."

LUCA:
"What, seriously?"

"It's just gone?"

BARRY *(his voice gains confidence as he warms to the topic):*
"Oh, no, that's not the best part."

MARC:
"Ya, they found the house."

LUCA:
"Did it reappear?"

BARRY:
"Ya, hundreds of miles away."

LUCA:
"No shit?" Like someone just…picked it up and moved it?"

BARRY and MARC *(speaking simultaneously):*
"Ya."

BARRY:
"Spirit orbs can be included as evidence, but most everyday people don't realize that orbs have to come in pairs. If they don't…it's probably dust."

LUCA:
"OK, I have never heard that."

"Why do you think that is?"

BARRY:
"Well, it's the behavior that tells you what it is, or isn't."

"If we look at all of the orb footage captured, you'll notice that only the orbs that come in pairs move in erratic ways."

"Floating around, nice and peaceful: speck of dust. And they too, can appear weird based on the air currents."

"But that's nothing like the behavior of the twin orbs. And we've seen that in person."

MARC:
"Yup."

LUCA:
"OK, that's wild, I want to see that. You guys have some of that footage?"

BARRY:
"Not on us, but we'll send you what we have."

LUCA:
"That would be awesome."

BARRY:
"Then there are the electronic phenomena such as EVP's that we record on digital recorders and play back later."

LUCA:
"Ya, we've heard plenty of those on the show. Do you use any tools to help stimulate the ghosts? That's pretty popular right now, especially with the EVP crowd."

MARC:
"Na, we don't go in for that kooky shit that supposedly picks

words out of the ether. That's crap."

LUCA:
"You gotta have your standards."

(Muffled grunting emanates from behind Luca again.)

LUCA:
"Sassy has made the prediction that this image represents the pinnacle of evidence you have gathered."

(Barry's chair creaks again.)

BARRY:
"Oh sure. It has been submitted for review, so it's still not widely accepted evidence yet. But, I mean, you've seen it."

LUCA:
"Yes, I have, and it is terrifying. So, let's get into it, Barry, your brush with certain death."

"Now, for our audio-only crowd, I will endeavor to describe the image to you, my faithful spooks."

"It's a wide shot of our protagonist, Barry. Across from Barry—certain doom."

"A moment of dark fate caught forever in digital. A testimony to the gigantic balls on the man sitting across from me."

(Beat. Soundboard: a single, slowed-down camera shutter. Then silence.)

LUCA *(casual, leaning in):*
"Alright, Barry. You've got the floor. Set the scene for us—what exactly happened in that tunnel?"

(Short pause. The sound of Barry exhaling slowly, the faint crack of a stiff joint or knuckle adjusting—subtle, unfamiliar in tone.)

BARRY *(soft, measured):*
"It started like any other sweep."

"Marc and I were tracking the usual anomalies—pressure fluctuations, sharp temperature spikes, magnetic disturbances. Nothing out of the ordinary for a place like that."

(Faint sound cue: distant metallic creaks and a low background thrum, as if descending deeper underground.)

BARRY *(cont'd):*
"But then the air shifted. Thick. Wet. Heavy."

"And it had this...taste. Like iron and something sweet—too sweet. Almost rotten sweet."

(Luca makes a quiet "hmm" sound but doesn't interrupt.)

BARRY:
"That's when the lights above us—ten in a row—cut out. All at once."

"No flicker. No dimming. Just...gone. Total blackness."

"And then we heard it. Breathing. Not near, but like, all around us. Like whatever it was had lungs bigger than the tunnel could hold."

"That's when the lights snap back on and…"

(Barry shudders at the memory.)

(Background: The faint, hollow sound of massive inhalation and exhalation echoes briefly.)

LUCA (playing it up, half-joking):
"So what's a seasoned explorer like yourself to do in a moment like that? Say a quick prayer? Look for the nearest exit sign?"

(Barry lets a small, humorless chuckle slip.)

BARRY:
"Marc raised the camera before I even knew what was happening. Reflex, maybe. He didn't aim. Just clicked."

"And then…right in front of me."

"The thing was standing there—closer than I'd realized."

"Eyes flat, dead. And they locked right on me."

(A tense silence stretches for a beat.)

LUCA (quieter now, as if leaning in):
"And then?"

(Barry's chair creaks slightly as he shifts his weight.)

BARRY:
"And then I hauled ass."

(Laughter breaks out from all three men.)

LUCA (*gestures over his shoulder*):
"Even Sassy liked that part."

(*The muffled sound of pounding results, causing more laughter from the men.*)

MARC:
"By the time we regrouped, it was gone. Like it had never been there."

(*Sound cue: A faint, sickening scrape, high-pitched and unnatural, fades in briefly and cuts out.*)

LUCA (*back to his bravado, covering his own discomfort*):
"Whew! Gives me goosebumps just hearing it. So, what'd you do then? Run for the hills?"

BARRY (*after a pause, voice soft*):
"You know it's funny…you do this job long enough, you find that you panic and run at the idea of encountering a monster, but when you do encounter a monster, you just have to know."

"And there are just too many things happening at once in a situation like that. Like I said, your mind is trying really hard to make everything you're seeing make sense, even though you know there is none."

"But you have to go back. No matter how scared you were a few minutes ago, no matter how scared you are in that moment; you are a paranormal investigator, so…you have to investigate what you saw."

(Barry throws his hands up in exasperation.)

MARC:
"I think what Barry's trying to say is…you don't get to choose what you do in that moment. I mean I didn't think about taking the picture right then, it was just what I do. Like I fell back on my training."

(Muffled grunting and pounding follows.)

LUCA *(nods over his shoulder):*
"Sassy wants to know if you pissed yourselves."

BARRY:
"No, not this time…wait, you can understand him?"

LUCA:
"Oh yeah, unfortunately."

(Muffled grunting and pounding from Sassy, mixed with a laugh track from the soundboard.)

LUCA:
"Was this the first time you've encountered something like this?"

BARRY:
"On this scale? Sure. I mean, when you've been at this long enough, you collect a lot of stories. But…ya, this was different."

MARC:
"A lot of hunters don't survive these encounters. Probably."

LUCA:
"Uh-huh."

"So, are you ready to retire? Does coming so close to…whatever these things are, and whatever they do to the unlucky hunters they encounter, it can't be good, does that maybe encourage you to 'hang it up' so to speak."

BARRY *(soft, measured):*
"Oh sure. You think about your family, at that moment. They say your life flashes before your eyes…it's like that, I understand what they mean, but it's a little different. Like…you have all this time, just in that moment. You know, like life and death just stop time while they sort you out."

LUCA:
"Dark. And deep, Barry. You're a man of unplumbed depths."

BARRY:
"Yeah."

(Barry lets a small, humorless chuckle slip.)

LUCA *(quieter now, as if leaning in):*
"Speaking of darkness, my chat is relentless, I must get to the meat. You've come face-to-face with one of these monsters, what

are they? What do they want? And most importantly…will they accept Sassy as a sacrifice?"

(Muffled pounding from Sassy.)

BARRY *(chuckles at the joke):*
"Well we know that they are everywhere; literally all over the world. They seem to be more common in urban environments, but stories have circulated for, well, forever about sightings in forests, deserts, swamps even in the oceans."

"There is still some debate over what exactly they are, even our picture doesn't answer as many questions as it raises."

LUCA:
"That is a good point, in fact didn't we run a poll in our chat? I think…can't seem to find it now that I want it. Dammit Sassy, do I have to do everything around here? Oh, there it is."

(Luca clears his throat.)

"Let's see what we got for the poll 'What the hell are these things?': It looks like Ghost won the poll at 33%; Demon second with 27%; Extraterrestrial placed third with 13%, Government experiment tied that with 13%, extra-dimensional being, I don't even know what that means, came in with 9% and Sassy's left nut came in last with 5%."

"So…looks like our chat is leaning toward these things being phantoms. Where does **PEEPS** fall in this discussion, because this is big right now, everyone has an opinion."

MARC *(bumps his mic as he leans in):*
"Ya, I even saw a politician somewhere made a bet that it would turn out to be a government experiment."

LUCA:
"Yeah, yeah, right, I saw that too."

BARRY *(leans in, but remains silent for a moment, arranging his thoughts):*
"It definitely felt demonic to me, and in our experience, these things often show up in groups, they are accompanied by foul odors, and they tend to be bullies, right?"

MARC *(bumps his mic as he leans in):*
"Ya, they are really demanding, some of our EVPs seem to start out pretty mellow, but if they don't get the response they are expecting...whoo."

LUCA *(nodding):*
"Interesting, very interesting. Marc if you bump that mic again, I'm taking it away from you."

MARC:
"Sorry."

LUCA *(nodding):*
"I swear it's just like having Sassy out here."

(Muffled grunting.)

"So, you're hanging in there? Looking for more of these things?"

BARRY:
"Ya, definitely, I think."

LUCA:
"We'll let chat help us out with that one, over the break I'll set up a poll on what chat thinks **PEEPS** should do next."

"And on that note, Barry, you wanna take us out for our first advertiser break? We'll pick up our conversation with **PEEPS** right after. Just say the line."

BARRY *(leans in and clears his throat.):*
"Hi, my name is Barry, and I came face-to-face with a human being; and lived to tell the tale."

ANNOUNCER (bright, smooth):

"This episode of *I Faced Certain Death; and Lived to Tell the Tale* is sponsored by ***BetterLair***—online therapy for creatures just trying to live their lives without being chased, cornered, or screamed at by humans."

"Because honestly? Existing in the dark is easy. Existing around people is the hard part. If you're exhausted from surprise flash photos, panicked investigators, or yet another night of 'What is that thing?!'...***BetterLair*** has counselors who get it."

"Use promo code **NOTAMONSTEROKAY** for 20% off your first month at www.monstersneedboundariestoo.com."

Eventide

Inspired by STORYFORGE: Advanced Horror Writing Prompts BOOK TWO

No prompt was provided, this was the cover image for Book
Two. Sometimes, the images can be even more inspiring than
the text prompts.

EVENTIDE

Chapter 1

Winter assailed the city with gusts of biting cold wind that cut through wool and caused bones to ache deep in the marrow. Early darkness prompted by the swollen and plunging storm clouds caused the day to feel even colder. Despite the raw conditions, New York City teemed with life and hustle as the people went about their business. Beneath the brooding presence of the Eventide—or, The Fischer Building, as it was formally known—on 43rd and Lexington, the streets were choked with motorcars and crowds of pedestrians.

The building rose above them like a monolith hewn from dusk itself. Towering forty-five stories above the cold, chaotic Manhattan streets, its red brick was weathered and veined with grime and soot. It was crowned with delicate spirelets that resembled flensed bones and scraped at the bruised underbelly of the swollen clouds. Its base resembled a fortress of dark granite; red lamplight flickered from deeply recessed windows.

Eventide narrowed as she rose from the dusky foundation, brick colored like old blood rose for most of her height before giving way to the final few floors. These were narrower still and wrapped in slabs of tarnished metal and an elaborate cresting of weathered copper. The curious framework of copper that enveloped the upper tower was famously known as Fischer's Crown and had secured the man and his building a place in history.

Beneath that gathering gloom, many people of wealth, curiosity or boredom swelled into crowds waiting to enter the dark building. Gleaming motorcars with polished brass fixtures rolled to a slow stop in front of the Eventide's great entrance, their passengers emerged like silk moths from lacquered chrysalises. Fur-trimmed coats, glinting cigarette holders, the white flash of gold and pearl—men and women drawn by the spectacle of haunted wonder. They all wore a certain half-expectant, half-mocking smile; few of them were new to this. They had come to parlay with the spirits of the dead, and to glean stories that would woo others over martinis the next evening.

Mary O'Shea arrived on the arm of William Kelly; her alabaster skin lit from a glow that emerged from within. Clear, glacial blue eyes likewise expressed warmth and laughter. She wore a silver dress under a champagne-colored coat, fox fur brushing the sharp line of her jaw. A pale cloche, strewn with pearls, sat smartly on her perfectly arranged auburn locks, even in the brutal gusts of winter's fury. Her mouth was a work of art from a master's brush, crimson lips curled as she smiled up at her escort.

He had shaved, much to her surprise. In the pale gaslight, Will Kelly looked younger than his thirty-one years. His classic good looks: strong jaw, high cheekbones, were on full display for her. She had often requested he shave, but she never thought he would, and the fact he had done so made Mary feel warm inside. The faint flush in his exposed cheek prompted her to reach up and caress his face.

Will took her hand in his with a tolerant smile, she might have already done this once. Or twice. His blue eyes met hers, and

MARY O'SHEA

WILLIAM KELLY

his hair, tousled and dark, curled like smoke in the cold wind. Mary looped her arm tighter around his. She tried to put her suspicions that Will was here for business out of her mind. Mary wanted tonight to be perfect. She wanted it to be about her.

"You didn't tell me you'd be making such a drastic change," she teased lightly.

"Needed a change," he said. "Anyway, I think it must make me appear more gullible for the lot we're about to rub elbows with."

"William Kelly!" Mary declared, striking the man's shoulder playfully. "You promised to behave, and not bully, arrest or shoot any of the spiritualists here tonight."

"And you believed me?" Will smiled slyly as he guided Mary between motorcars and through the crowd gathered around Eventide's grand entrance.

Mary responded with a wry smile; she put her hand to her cloche to keep it seated on her ginger curls as a chilly gust rocked them. A commotion among the onlookers snared her attention. Several sleek, black motorcars passed the entrance and turned into the alley beside the building. Mary craned her neck in hopes of catching sight of one of the famous spiritualists arriving, but Will moved her forward toward the entrance.

The crowd quickly consumed them. The doormen, clad in red and black livery, resembled soldiers guarding the gleaming brass doors. Slowly, inexorably, they were drawn into the maw of the great bloodstained monolith. The atmosphere was bright and cheerful, despite the bitter cold, and many friends and acquaintances met and caught up or gossiped about the night's entertainment. There was, it was said, a surprise guest tonight, and the public was awash in curiosity.

A figure moved quickly past. A streak of gloom in the pale air. The thin woman in mourning black passed immediately behind Will and Mary as she made her way toward the alley. She would certainly have recognized Will Kelly on sight, had the Pinkerton Agent not shaved his beard.

Carla wore a dark veil that obscured her eyes and nose, preventing anyone from identifying her. A precaution she had taken due to the proliferation of her likeness in newspapers across the city. Her ministrations served her well, and she slipped unnoticed into the shadows of the alley.

* * *

The rear entrance of the Eventide had never been intended to host any pomp or pageantry, and yet tonight it did just that. Along the narrow street behind the grand tower, flanked by flickering arc-lamps, a second crowd had formed—smaller, stranger, and far more devout. These were not casual thrill-seekers. Nor were they socialites, out seeking a new thrill, or a fresh tale for the eager ears at the Club.

These people were a blend of true believers and committed skeptics. A tangled patchwork of spiritual zeal and worldly agnosticism. They chafed from the combination of bone chill and rising anticipation as the motorcars began to arrive. Whispers rose to a murmur, and the crowds constricted, fighting to close the gap between themselves and the famous spiritualists by inches. But one above all others drew this crowd on such a bitter night.

The first of the ebon town cars pulled up and a stout woman with cherubic face and large eyes stepped out. She was covered in colorful and elaborate scarves that were hand-painted with occult symbols and devices. Her fingers clinked and glittered with crystals as she lifted her arms to the crowd like a prize fighter. The response from the crowd was polite if unenthusiastic.

Another dark motorcar coasted to a stop as the previous one pulled away. A tall, weathered man with heavy, black eyeliner unfolded from the back seat. His wine-colored robes at odds with the black, velvet cage that held his animal spirit guide.

The procession continued. There were the Canary sisters, mediums from Baltimore. Johann Baptiste, the famous mesmerist lately of Berlin, and a boy-prophet who was making his debut tonight. While he was too young to shave, all agreed he possessed an old soul. Then a murmur rippled through the crowd that left a stillness in its wake.

A long black motorcar slid into place smoothly. Its windows gleamed like polished obsidian. The large door opened slowly. The crowd waited in breathless anticipation.

Gallo Santoro stepped from the car and surveyed the crowd. An Italian man in his fifties, Gallo was neither handsome, nor was he ugly. He was neat, and his tailored evening coat draped over his frame with theatrical precision. Beneath it, a brocade vest of violet with a pattern of a deeper hue, caught the light like bruised velvet.

Gallo toyed with a gold medallion attached to his vest out of habit as his eyes took in the crowd. He paused on certain faces, perhaps making notes in his mind. Then, seemingly content with all he had observed, the man turned his attention back to the motorcar.

GALLO SANTARO

ENZO SANTARO

Gallo held a gloved hand to receive a smaller, slimmer hand in a black glove. The crowd moved forward, necks straining.

Katia Santoro—the Angel of Vengeance, rose from the car.

She wore a gown of deepest midnight, fabric matte and heavy. Long, dark hair fell in waves from a simple, yet elegant headdress of black silk attached to metal bands in interwoven loops and symmetrical arcs. Each of the loops cradled a jet-black stone. The Angel wore no bangles, displayed no mystic coins or artifacts, there was no tinkling of charms as she moved. Her power did not depend on such conventions.

Her dark eyes were obscured behind round black glasses, complete with narrow blinders that blocked her peripheral vision entirely. To the crowd, she appeared blind and relied upon her uncle for direction. Gallo leaned close and whispered something, his hand still held hers. Her effect on the crowd was immediate. There was no cheering from fans or jeering from detractors. A quiet hush fell over the alley and remained.

Enzo Santoro emerged last, tall and sharp in a suit more contemporary than his father's, his handsome face showed an expression that was both anxious and protective. His hand found Katia's elbow, and he too whispered something to the young woman. Gallo carefully adjusted her shawl, then nodded once. Together, the men guided her up the shallow steps toward the service entrance beneath the crimson awning.

The cameras clicked only once—just once as she made her way past. The photographers seemed unable, or unwilling, to break the spell she had cast over the crowd. Katia did not speak. She did not wave. The crowd parted for her; some even bowed their heads as she passed.

KATIA SANTARO

Katia paused only once. She stared at the great building as if she sensed something. A sharp wind stirred her hair. Gallo touched her back. Enzo murmured something low and urgent in Italian. She moved again and the door closed behind her.

The Angel of Vengeance had entered the Eventide.

* * *

Beneath the jutting iron awning of an abandoned fruit stand, half-shrouded in evening shadow, Carla Rios watched the Angel of Vengeance. Icy wind teased her veil in gentle flicks, revealing only a fragment of her face at a time: a painted cheekbone, the fringe of her crimson lips, the cut of her jaw. Gusts periodically tore at the ebon mourning hat, but thick spined hairpins held firm against the buffeting cold. To any observer, she was just another devotee, cloaked in mourning and desperate hope.

A closer examination, however, repudiated such an inference. Carla didn't fidget like the others gathered in the alley. She waited patiently, never shifting her weight, or hugging herself in the crisp air. Unmoving, like a predator that understands her prey had no recourse but to venture within reach of her strike. Carla's eyes, sharp and dark behind the veil, focused on the tall black motorcar that glided to a stop.

First the tramp's uncle exited and primped himself. And then she stepped out. Bile rose in Carla's throat at the sight of the medium; she would never refer to Katia Santoro as an angel. Only a demon. A demon who stole everything from Carla, even her future. Especially her future. Her face splashed on tabloids across the

CARLA RIOS

world, and her name was linked to a capital crime. Carla would make her pay.

The crowd quieted as Katia passed by aided by her uncle and cousin. Carla's lips parted behind the veil and a low hiss escaped. It was all theater, the glasses—she was not blind! All these fools who watched in awe as she shuffled past, as if she were somehow infirm. But they were the blind ones, those who bowed their heads in reverence for her imagined power.

Once, Carla had wanted to know how; how had this charlatan known so much about her? Or her lover? Or their crime—no, his crime she corrected herself. Carla may have planned it, encouraged it, and made threats if she didn't get what she wanted. But she didn't kill anyone. Not really. It simply wasn't the same thing, Carla reassured herself.

She told herself she no longer cared how Katia had acquired the intimate details, for in truth there could be only one way. Carla didn't believe in magic or miracles, gods or devils, she believed in herself. That meant the only way Katia could know the private details between Carla and her lover is if Katia had crept into his bed as well. Like an alley cat. Carla paused her mental tirade to spit. She would deal with this slut herself.

She watched Katia move through the alley like some divine prophet—led gently by a man Carla recognized as the cousin, flanked by the uncle. Katia, wrapped in black like a widow who hadn't earned the right to mourn, not like Carla had. Her lovely face twisted at the thought, and she unconsciously slid a gloved hand into her slim, dark leather purse.

It felt like ice. Even despite the cold gusts of the coming winter, even when compared to her broken, torn heart, the revolver was colder still. A relic of her family, the 7mm pin-fire pistol was an antique, but it was dependable. If she was close enough to her victim. And if she could get even closer to the demon…Carla released the pistol and raised her hand to her lips, kissing her mother's ring beneath the fabric.

No. It would not end in an alley on a cold evening. Carla would execute Katia Santoro while she sat on her throne, holding court with fools and mountebanks. Katia would remove those damned glasses and look Carla in the eyes as she put a bullet through the medium's skull. She would expose their Angel for the fraud that she was. Then she would have justice. For herself. For her lover.

Carla stepped back into deeper shadow, turning her face away from the spectacle. She took several sharp, shuddering breaths. Then she turned and walked out of the alley. Moving with renewed purpose, the veil fluttering against her cheeks, boots clipping smartly on the pavement. A crisp gust swirled dead leaves about her ankles as she turned the corner and made her way toward the grand entrance of the Eventide. Spotlights painted the tower's high walls in flame and blood, which suited her mood. She approached the front steps not as a curious guest, not as an inane worshiper of the dead—but as an emissary of death itself.

The doormen barely noticed her, seeing another fashionably odd woman among dozens.

The invitation she presented was in the name of a dead man, but they didn't notice. Carla proceeded into a wall of warmth and smells, as if her nose had suddenly thawed. A steward offered her a hand and guided Carla up the thick, vermilion carpeted steps.

Carla Rios entered the Eventide with a singular focus: Tonight, the Angel of Vengeance would truly make contact with the dead.

Chapter 2

The grand atrium was abuzz. Mary passed off her hat and fur to a young man dressed in hotel livery. Will declined the offer; he wore no hat and chose to retain his coat. Above them, the tower's vaulted atrium stretched into shadow, a cage of glass and gold. And all about, a sea of silk, fur and precious stones churned.

Distant music occasionally bobbed above the surface of the clamorous crowd. Bix Beiderbecke-style cornet, high and sweet atop a rhythmic web of drums and piano drew Will's attention. He placed a hand on Mary's lower back and guided her around the edge of the human morass. When she heard the band, she perked up.

"Oh, no," she shook her head but allowed Will to continue guiding her. "If we start dancing now, we won't stop in time for the séance."

Will smiled in return. "Okay, no dancing. But the crowd must thin a bit at the club."

The air thickened with perfume and tobacco smoke as they approached The Eventide Club. Couples jitterbugged and Charlestoned across the scarlet and black tiles. Bobbed hair and feathers dominated this crowd.

Woman wore dresses that clung like smoke and were sliced scandalously low at the back. Men in tuxedos crouched like wolves at the bar, double-breasted and diamond-pinned, their eyes gleamed with drink and desire.

LOWER TOWER LIVERY

Cigarettes in long ivory holders dangled from fingers that cast back light in a shower of sparks. Gold and gemmed cuff links glinted like the eyes of a predator. Wait staff passed by with flutes of illegal champagne and a young woman giggled loud enough to scandalize party goers across the dance floor. William stopped short of the kitchens.

"Are you hungry?" Mary inquired.

Will stared for a moment, thinking to himself.

"No," he chuckled, "of course not."

Mary opened her mouth to say something when her attention was snared by something behind him. Will turned and noticed activity on the great mezzanine of the third floor that overlooked the crowd. Mary snatched his hand and pulled.

"Come on, Will, it's starting."

A brief look of regret flashed across the man's face, then he smiled and allowed himself to be dragged back into the crowd.

* * *

The Herald arrived on the forty-fifth floor. He was a tall man with sharp and deliberate features. His mouth was a thin line, only suited for the speaking of solemn, weighty matters. The man's attire was impeccable: a black tuxedo jacket that molded to his square shoulders, a perfectly knotted bow tie rode against a high-collared white shirt. Beneath that he wore textured waistcoat in charcoal tones with swirling patterns.

THE HERALD

His walnut-dark hair was parted with precision, with a light dusting of silver at his temples. His eyes were wide, grey and empty. He stood still with only the occasional twitch of a muscle around his eyes and mouth. A moment later his fingers began to twitch, and two men in the crimson livery of the Eventide approached him.

One of the men reached out a hand and took hold of the Herald by a bicep. The two men went still again. A few moments later the Heralds eyes cleared, and he began to move his head around, taking in the room and the two men that flanked him. Releasing the man's arm, the first uniformed stranger stepped back and spoke.

"Welcome to the Eventide, this way, the Queen is waiting."

With that said, the men turned and began walking.

The Herald stumbled after them, slowly gaining his balance like a clumsy colt, walking for the first time. The men did not appear surprised or concerned, nor did they reach out to assist or steady the Herald. By the time the trio had descended the narrow flight of steps their guest had gained his bearings, though he still lagged, examining rug, carpet or painting. The furniture piqued his fancy too, and he had to sit in every divan and chair they passed, inspect every velvet-lined antechamber.

"It's so warm here," his face twisted in a macabre parody of a smile. "It's wonderful."

The two escorts replied with genuine smiles.

"We are gratified that you approve, Herald. However, we should not keep the Queen waiting."

Grudgingly the man rose and resumed following the men but still failed to keep pace effectively. There was just too much to examine. After a brief eternity the group reached a bank of three crimson elevators. Here their company encountered more delays when the Herald discovered the elevator's buttons.

* * *

The music in the grand atrium of The Eventide fell away like a curtain being drawn. A hush moved through the crowd, rippling outward from the crimson-carpeted marble stairs even permeating the riotous flappers on the dance floor who quietly turned toward the great balcony. The throng stared as a single golden spotlight bloomed from the dome, striking the center of the mezzanine like the sun parting night.

The mezzanine itself, gilded and vaulted, cast a half-circle over the room like the balcony of a great opera house. From this height, one could see all—the polished heads of industrial barons, the opal necklaces of widowed heiresses, the wide eyes of society's curious daughters and their bored, gin-soused mothers. A low hum rose briefly as a figure entered the pool of shining light.

Ester Fischer, better known by her stage name, Queen Carlotta, stepped up to the balcony. The woman's royal title was an affectation, but one would never know it by seeing her. The Queen of the Eventide exuded an imperial intensity that bordered on unnatural, as if she had been born a monarch. She drew attention like a black hole; nothing escaped, and all movement and sound ceased at her gaze.

Her hair, dark as night and gleaming, was drawn back and held beneath an opulent crown. Ancient in design, it was an intricately wrought piece, festooned with red stones and filigreed metal. It gave one the impression that it was a holy relic rather than a bit of jewelry. The central jewel glowed blood-bright and rested at the center of her brow like a third eye. Her veil, sheer and sable, was edged in gold embroidery that caught the light like ribbons of stars.

Necklaces, heavy with pearls and rubies, were layered about her neck and arranged for ceremony rather than decoration. Every element of her attire—the sculpted earrings, the symmetry of her dress, the deep red fabric slashed with black and bronze, all spoke of ritual and power in perfect balance. Her lips, painted a rich and decisive red, curled into an elegant smile. Then she spoke, and her voice, rich and melodious, charmed her subjects.

"My beloved guests…seekers, skeptics, and supplicants alike…" Her accent was foreign, but time-worn, bent into the curvature of stagecraft. "Welcome to the Eventide."

A gentle applause rustled through the crowd.

"You have come in search of truth," she said, her gaze sweeping across the assembled faces below. "Of knowledge. Of mercy. Of justice. And tonight, the veil may thin for those truly worthy. For here, in this sacred tower—this stairway carved from faith and will—we are closer to the beyond than any other place in our world."

She spread her arms to encompass the whole of the atrium, her fingers alight with a riot of reflections from her many gold and jeweled rings.

QUEEN CARLOTTA

"Whatever it is that you seek, no matter the barriers or tribulations you may perceive, we can aid you."

Carlotta turned to her right, and with her raised arm gestured.

A slender woman draped in a flowing veil of marigold silk over violet robes winking with gold thread stepped forward. Her face was serene, and her head bowed slightly in supplication.

"To my right," Carlotta intoned, "the divine vessel of the Kashmiri winds. Asha Manna, the Eye of Kashmir, will cast your petitions before the spirits of earth and sky."

Again, a gentle applause rose from the atrium.

"And to my left," Carlotta continued, "I present to you a voice of the ancestors, a speaker for the spirits of blood and bone. Priestess Urha Kane, who tonight joins our ranks—not as a guest, but as kin."

Her garments ablaze with color; hues of deep saffron and burnt ochre layered with rich, organic textures, Uhra Kane stepped into the light. The woman stood with the quiet authority of someone who has long since stopped asking for permission. Her dark skin was carved in wisdom's image, lined not by age alone but by consequence. Her eyes—half-lidded, steady— gleamed with a keen intelligence.

Applause now. A bit heartier, fueled by the crowd's expectation.

But Carlotta waited. She let the tension build in silence.

"And…as a special delight," She smiled now, sensing that many in the crowd had already guessed her surprise. "There is another. A rare flower…whose power is rooted not in the

ASHA MANNA

URHA KANE

elements, nor in ancestry, but in death. You know her name, you have seen it in the gazettes. She revealed a killer with the testimony of a ghost...the victim's ghost in fact, and brought justice to the aggrieved."

The Queen allowed realization to ripple through the crowd for a few breaths.

"I speak, of course, of *The Angel of Vengeance.*"

A second wave of whispers, gasps, and one audible "She's here?" Passed though the assembly.

Carlotta raised her hands higher.

"Welcome to the Eventide," she decreed. "Let the spirits be kind...and all your wishes fulfilled!"

The applause came like thunder.

The Herald stepped up to greet Queen Carlotta as she cast one last smile to the cheering crowd and turned away. She walked past him without so much as a glance, and the crimson-clad escorts motioned for him to follow the woman into the elevator.

Queen Carlotta waited for the Herald to join her. The doors closed leaving them in nearly total quiet.

The silence persisted as the elevator rose quickly toward the highest part of the Eventide. The psychomanteum they called it. A place that stretched the veil so thin, even the most unseasoned medium could contact a spirit. The place from which Carlotta oversaw her domain. Enthroned in a New York penthouse.

The Herald merely studied the Queen as the elevator raced to the sky. He looked down at her hand resting against the brass rail. He had often been praised for his boldness, so he decided to follow his instincts. He reached for her hand. Carlotta glared at him even as he reached out.

The Herald recoiled quickly. "I—I thought it would be more efficient."

"Not here. Never here." Her voice, still low and silky, carried a definite edge. Her eyes pinned him in place as Carlotta stepped closer, closing the distance with a cold authority that made the car of the lift feel much too small.

"You thought wrong. Our place here is precarious, as you well know. Is that not your purpose here? To convey to me the fears of your betters?"

He lowered his gaze, blinking again, his smile faltering. "I apologize. Yes," he looked up to meet her gaze, "we have many concerns about the operation."

"*My* operation," she corrected, then moved away again.

There was silence, the lift rising steadily, the sound of its gears soft as whispers.

At last, he nodded, conceding her point. "We have no intention of changing that fact."

Carlotta arched an eyebrow.

"We don't wish to challenge your authority," the Herald said, more gently now. "We want to work with you."

She stared at him for several seconds, her expression cool but ultimately unreadable, as though considering the likelihood he could be trusted, and perhaps whether she even cared.

Then—ding. The doors opened.

Without a word, she stepped out onto the upper floor and addressed two of her men in the red uniform.

"Give our guest the tour," she graced him with one last dispassionate look, then turned and walked away. "Then bring him to the observation chamber."

The men bowed their heads to their queen's back, then motioned for him to return to the lift. The Herald complied.

* * *

Mary had stiffened at the mention of Katia Santoro's stage name. By the time the Queen had finished her speech, there was enough room between her and Will for a waiter to pass through. A long, uncomfortable silence stretched between them until the applause died down enough so one could be heard. Mary spoke first.

"Fancy that, Will," she didn't look at him, couldn't look at him. "Your childhood sweetheart performing here tonight. What a happy coincidence for you."

"Mary," Will pleaded. He reached for her, but she stepped beyond his range. "Let me explain."

"No…" she stumbled over her thoughts for a moment, then decided to be honest. "No, Will, no. I don't want you to explain, because you may have a very good reason for using me tonight, but I don't want to hear it. I want to be angry for a while."

Mary walked away casting back, "Alone", over her shoulder as she made her way toward the stairway that led to the mezzanine.

The crowd thinned significantly the nearer she came to the white and scarlet steps that led up to the great balcony. The elevators on the mezzanine led to the famous psychomanteum, where the wealthiest of clients held séance or divination. Mary's name, O'Shea, opened doors around the world for her, and the Eventide was no different. The dark uniformed porter assured her there would be no problem with her joining the Angel's party and kindly escorted her to an elevator.

The crowd broke around Carla like waves. Some murmured softly, excusing themselves, others spoke a bit louder, and remarked on her rudeness. She heard none of this. Her gaze, secreted beneath the veil, held only Mary O'Shea.

Everyone knew Mary O'Shea, everywhere she went. Everywhere Carla went. Her eyes expertly appraised the pearls—genuine, the flashes from the stones on her fingers were dazzling. They were real too.

Carla hated the woman because of what she had, all that she had. Carla should have these things; she deserved them more. Mary had never known hunger, not really. She had never had to sleep on soiled earth, because exhaustion had removed any choice. Carla stretched credulity a bit on the suffering of her past. Increasingly so, each time she repeated these grievances to herself.

She seethed quietly, a kettle just before release, as the ebon clad man escorted Mary to an elevator and waited to see her off. The unfairness of it all quickly overwhelmed her, and she sought to retrieve a lace tissue from her purse. But her hand brushed the cold metal of the pistol, and an icy calm settled over her. Once she was through with the hex-hustling slut, Carla could take what she wanted from Mary next.

Why not? She deserved it. Carla deserved all of it.

She strode forward with renewed purpose. At the top of the stairs, she too was greeted by a porter in the hotel's dark livery. She presented an introduction card from one of her previous employers. Too wealthy and powerful to risk turning her away, or so she thought.

"I'm sorry ma'am," he apologized sincerely, "but there is no more room on the schedule for The Angel. Perhaps you might find the Eye of Kashmir as satisfying?"

Carla contemplated quietly for a breath.

"Are they on the same floor?" She asked.

"Yes, the 42nd floor." He confirmed.

"Good, send me to the 42nd floor, I will do the rest."

A brief look of confusion passed his face, then he smiled and held out an arm toward the elevators.

"This way, Please, ma'am."

SERVER

Chapter 3

Will watched Mary until the elevator doors closed. She was right, if Will had told Mary the truth from the start she would absolutely have helped. And she would absolutely have insisted on going along. He'd expected her to be angry, but he had not expected her to seek out Kat. Now Will had to protect both women.

Will began walking quickly. He wended his way through the crowd, making a gradual curve for the dancing. Mary had been suspicious from the start, Will was a Pinkerton agent, a dyed-in-the-wool pragmatist. He did not believe in mediums or spirits, and he never would. Mary hadn't questioned his motives when he invited himself along. She had just been pleased to spend the evening with Will anywhere. He would have to make this up to her somehow.

William also did not believe in coincidence. So, when Carla Rios slipped her police tail and missed her court-ordered check-in, Will had a bad feeling in his gut. He knew that Kat and her family had arrived in the city for a performance at the Eventide, so it stood to reason that Carla had heard the same news. Will doubted that anyone alive could even count the number of times the fiery Spanish woman had threatened to murder Kat, and he took her threat as deadly serious.

He turned sharply as the flappers thickened, rounding the perimeter of the nightclub. Soon the smell of frying meat made his stomach rumble, and the temperature rose a few degrees as he neared the kitchens. Just past the coat-check for the nightclub entrance he spied the man he was looking for.

LUTHER FULLER

Luther Fuller had a hard, sunken face. As if carved from stone, it carried the deep-etched lines of someone who smiled only to mask a threat. His skin was weathered by a lifetime of exposure to harsh climates and worse associates. His eyes—pale and sharp as ice—clocked Will the moment he appeared. Fuller didn't move, only adjusted the gloves on his hands and gave a slight, professional nod.

He wore the Eventide's charcoal uniform well, gold-threaded epaulets catching the low light, Will had to admit the uniform hid a lot of dirt. He stopped directly beside the bootlegger. Will held out a small glass bottle of whiskey. He didn't like dealing with the likes of Luther, in fact he believed the world would be a brighter place if Luther Fuller was incarcerated or dead. But Kat was in danger, so no line would be too far.

Luther extended his gloved hand and took the flask with a flick of his wrist, thumbing the cap off without ceremony. The scent hit him first. He took a small sip. Held it. Swallowed. He remained silent, but nodded urgently, then took another sip.

Will carefully removed his overcoat and held it out for Luther to inspect. The man ran a hand along the coat, feeling the three additional flasks agreed upon. Luther took the overcoat then, and bobbed it in his hand a few times, judging the weight. Then satisfied, he nodded and reached into his coat and drew out a small envelope and offered it to the agent.

Will slipped the envelope into his inner pocket and, without a word, walked away from Luther back toward the coat check for The Eventide's club entrance. The counter was carved from ebon wood, lacquered to a gloss, and fronted with an elegant bronze grillwork. Behind it stood a clerk, thin and colorless, but alert. A white carnation in his lapel twitched slightly with each breath.

Will slid the envelope he received from Fuller across the counter. The thin man took it, and with a practiced nod, broke the seal beneath the counter's edge. Inside was a single ticket: a number hand-penned in dark graphite—sharp, slanted, deliberate. The clerk's expression did not change, but he paused for a moment before disappearing behind a pair of velvet drapes.

The clerk emerged with a long, narrow box wrapped in brown paper and secured with black twine, atop a fabric bundle. The parcel was unmarked except for one corner where the stamp of the Eventide mail room had been placed. The bundle proved to be a sable uniform for the Eventide including a hat. If the clerk had any opinion on a strange man arriving with a ticket that accessed an unknown parcel and a uniform, it did not reach his face.

"Could I trouble you for a pen?" Asked Will.

The slender clerk provided one for him, and he wrote the name 'Professor Lucien Virelli' on the package. Will had kept the man's identity to himself. There was no way he would let Fuller know that Pinkerton had a shadow agent in the Eventide. He returned the pen to his stoic witness, donned the jacket and hat and snatched the parcel. Will thanked the man and turned away, fastening the buttons on the jacket as he walked.

Once more he waded into the swell of humanity, this time headed for the registration desk. When he arrived, he chose a young woman at the end of the long, wooden desk, away from the others.

"Hello, beautiful," he rested an arm on the counter.

Her surprise turned into a smile when she looked up at Will.

"Hello…"

"Will, nice to meet you…"

"Lucy." She supplied it with a blush.

"You know," he leaned in conspiratorially, "I'm not with them."

She followed his nod toward the guests for the evening's festivities, then looked back at him confused.

"I don't have a spirit guide." He held up the parcel, a name without an address.

She took the package and found the stamp.

"How did that happen?" She smiled and held up a finger, then moved away and consulted a ledger. She scratched out the address with a pen then returned the package.

"Here you go, Will," her smile widened. "I'm very sorry about that. If you think of a way I can make it up to you…"

"Oh, Lucy," he grinned, "you can count on that."

Will turned away and headed for the nearest staff access. He passed through the outer door to encounter a second door just beyond. This one bore a sign that read 'Tower Access – Staff Only – Authorized Personnel'. A second, smaller sign beneath it read: 'Deliveries to the Psychomanteum Must Be Cleared Through Security'.

Two bored young men in black stood guard, and once they

located the stamp on the parcel, they opened the door and waved Will through. He passed down a long hallway, making his way from memory. He had studied everything he could find on the Eventide, floor plan included, but he had not accounted for the effect such an event had on the staff. He was shocked by the number of employees required to manage the guests' needs. The staff elevators were crowded with maids, porters and pages all trying to get to the upper floors. Will screwed up his face and looked at the parcel again, maybe he had read it wrong.

Nope. Apt No. 3503.

"Shit," Will exhaled as he abandoned the lift and began a search for the stairs.

Chapter 4

Mary followed her party from the elevator to the 42nd floor. She had never been to the psychomanteum before, and it lived up to its reputation. It was warm and dark and laden with mystery. It truly did feel like another world. The thick, rich carpets, the hue of blood absorbed all sound, and invited silence among the group. Mary thought she smelled something electrical as they made their way to the séance, it reminded her of a thunderstorm.

The Chamber of Endless Sight was Queen Carlotta's personal summoning room. It was circular and windowless, paneled in lacquered wood so dark it seemed to devour light. Despite the best efforts of the chandelier overhead—a bouquet of strange, translucent bulbs—it remained a dim, shadowy place. Befitting its ghostly purpose.

A massive oval rug sprawled at its center, the weaves of which were so dense and abstract it almost appeared to writhe in the dim light. The ceiling of the room vaulted into a shadowed hollow, causing the chamber to feel much larger than it was. In fact, the room seemed designed to defeat any attempt to define it.

Opposite the doors, on the far wall the room held a mirror. It rose at least ten feet in height, an oval monolith of black glass. Its obsidian frame was curled and folded with motifs of flame, eye, and some form resembling a serpent. Mary caught a glimpse of herself and the others upon entering, but the gloomy reflection it cast felt somehow…wrong. She studiously avoided looking at the mirror after that.

The large table filled the room, a narrow oval with clipped ends. Crafted from ebony, polished to a mirror finish, and devoid of ornament or decoration. No candles or salt. No ceremonial charms or crystals marred the table's perfect surface. Seven black chairs were spaced evenly on each side of the table, flanking the medium's throne.

Mary sat herself quietly to one side of the room, smiling in response to the low murmurs of greeting from the other guests. Slowly, reverently, the party found seats around the table or walls. Only then did the old woman enter, escorted by several crimson porters. Once she was settled in the great chair before the mirror, the men departed and sealed the room.

Babi Ester—or Granny Ester—wore a patchwork robe that appeared to have been stitched together from the trappings of six empires and at least three lifetimes. Beads and bangles shimmered at her wrists. Her many necklaces chimed when she moved like tiny bells. She wore a head-wrap that was a garish amalgam of coins and cloth that seemed to move slightly when she tilted her head, as though it was about to topple off.

She looked up at the assembled group and smiled. It was an honest smile, not the opening pitch of a fraud or a showman, and the others, Mary included, could not help themselves from returning their own smiles to the medium. Babi Ester smiled like a woman who remembered what it was to be a child, and to feel the thrill of taking a road of discovery. The satisfaction that came with something new. And she sought it out with the same dramatic flourish as the clothes she wore.

Babi Ester pulled a roll of velvet from her loose robes. The fabric was wine-colored and worn at the edges. She carefully placed this on the table, then from another hidden pocket, produced four, smooth river rocks. The stones she placed on the velvet cloth; one at each corner to hold it in place. Then the old woman produced a small bag that was bedecked with curious charms and bits of bone.

Granny Ester whispered a quiet invocation as she dumped the bag over the velvet. Her rune stones spilled into a small pile, and she paused to inspect the work. Satisfied the spirits were indeed pacified by her prayer, she deliberately dragged a hand across the mound, spreading the stones thin. Then she looked up at the assembly and smiled again.

"Blessings on this chamber and those gathered to honor the runes," Ester said, her voice sweet and rasping, like water poured over gravel. "And blessings upon those souls brave enough to sit in it."

A chuckle passed through the devotees. One man crossed himself. Another coughed.

Ester did not ask any names or inquire of anyone in the group their desire. She scooped up the runes in both hands, muttered something in a tongue that might have been Old Church Slavonic, and cast the stones back unto the table.

They landed with a series of soft clicks—deadened by the fabric. One after another, they fell into a loose spiral. The scattering should have been random. It was not. The symbols stared up from the table in patterns that were clear to see, even for the uninitiated at the table.

Ester's eyes fluttered closed. Her lips moved, mouthing words with no voice. Then she raised one hand, trembling, and hovered her fingers above the central rune. Suddenly the stone flipped by itself.

Several guests gasped in astonishment.

A breeze brushed their ankles—though no visible windows, vents, or cracks breached the room. The air had changed, subtly and undeniably. It smelled… wrong. Ozone, old dust, and honey.

Ester inhaled sharply. Her eyes opened. But gone was the grandmotherly warmth, the playful cunning. What her gaze now held was emotionless and cold. A tool of the spirits, given to truth, single-minded and unyielding.

This new Ester seemed to look through the people seated around, and several guests squirmed under her calculating gaze. When she spoke, her voice was deeper than before. And her words carried an accent that no one in the room could place.

"I sense many, many questions," she stated, "but the runes choose who they speak for, just as they choose who they speak through."

She threw her head back and placed her hand above the scattered stones.

"I sense, a lost one," her voice rose. "Young, oh no, dear no. I sense a young man. So young, he died in a war perhaps?"

Several sharp intakes of breath sounded, and Babi Ester began her séance.

On the other side of the dark mirror that served as the medium's backdrop, lay the Observation Room. From this vantage Queen Carlotta watched the séance unfold. She had seen the old woman perform before and had little interest in the show itself.

Instead, her gaze fell upon Mary O'Shea.

The dusky glass held the dimmed vision of the heiress, and suspended next to her, Carlotta's own reflection. Mary was held up by society as one of the most beautiful women in New York. Carlotta, too, was considered beautiful, but she was an aging star, and Mary was so young and bright.

As she observed the glow that seemed to emanate from the young woman, so much vitality and life within the confines of her mortal coil. What was this? Was this the human soul so many mediums sought to contact? Why did Mary shine brighter than Babi Ester—a spiritualist of such renown? This wasn't the first time Carlotta observed more vigor from the audience than the supposed mystics themselves.

It brought back a memory.

Years ago, the Queen had a conversation with a Sufi mystic who spoke of a concept completely alien to her. Predestination. The belief that a path was laid out for everyone, long before they took their first steps. That certain events or outcomes came to pass no matter how much they endeavored to avoid them.

At the time it sounded like a convenient excuse for their failures. One more delusion that allowed people to consider themselves special, unique, even necessary to the universe. And when something inevitably went wrong, they were free to blame their pre-charted course. The path laid out before their birth, something they had no control over.

It was never their fault.

Carlotta did not tolerate failure in herself or any that served her so she had closed her mind to the concept. Now something was forcing that idea upon her again, like a wound that burned for attention.

The Angel of Vengeance. That was when it had started. The Queen had passed the young woman briefly while both were on the mezzanine. It had left Carlotta with a single overriding thought that put all she knew up for debate.

The Angel was different. Not like the plump, old woman on the other side of the massive mirror. Not like the Eye of Kashmir, or Priestess Kane. Or herself.

A true medium, not just lucky guesses or a clever routine. She needed no one in the crowd to help sell her act to the gullible. In fact, Katia Santoro held the same power as the desperate and aggrieved that came seeking answers from the spiritualists. Only in an intensity the Queen had heretofore never witnessed.

This was what Carlotta sought, this genuine gift that set the Angel apart from the endless wave of humanity that broke over the Eventide. A power that the Queen could see herself wielding.

Predestination. Maybe this power was being laid right at her feet.

Curiosity had originally prompted her to invite Katia Santaro to The Eventide. That and the Angel's sudden fame in occult circles, and the droves of adherents that followed in her wake. But now, the Queen was uncertain if she would ever allow the woman to leave.

Chapter 5

The herald had surveyed the crowds from the balcony on the mezzanine, as close as the man wished to get. He was fascinated by the music and dancing but eschewed further investigation due to the press of humanity. So, his escorts took him higher into the tower.

The mid-tower, he learned, had been turned over as homes for dozens of occult practitioners by order of the Queen. They lived rent free, or so they believed. In truth, they were as much a part of Carlotta's operation as anyone in the psychomanteum. And they unknowingly served her day and night.

From mediums with spirit guides to witches who claimed to brew potions dear and dire, the Herald observed them all. Theosophists who proselytized the coming 'New Age', astrologers with beautiful and intricate star maps that the Herald made note to commandeer before his impending departure. Diviners who stared deeply into bowls of water, and sorcerers that burned pungent bits of plant and spice on small metal braziers. The Herald was very intrigued by the tarot cards, and how much variation one could find from one deck to the next.

He approved of the bone dice, carved from human bone under a new moon with a copper knife forged during an eclipse. But he drew the line at divining facts from spent tea leaves. He found this act ridiculous and said so. If not for the crimson clothed guides the Herald might not have returned from his tour a whole man. At last, it was decided to move the Herald along before someone was injured.

Later, in the psychomanteum, the Herald lay his face on the inner wall of the building.

"You're right, I can feel it," he remarked to his guides.

"It all passes through the core of the building," one of the men explained. "All thanks to Mr. Fischer."

"Yes, but...how?" The Herald pressed.

The man shook his head, "you'll have to ask the Queen that."

The man motioned for the Herald to resume their walk down the warm hallway.

"The Eye of Kashmir, or the Priestess Kane?" His guide stated their options.

The Herald mused for a moment, "the Priestess Kane, I think."

The man nodded and the small group passed by a room flanked by porters in scarlet labeled 'The Chamber of Still Waters'. They stopped before another room, this one held a sign on the doors that read 'The Chamber of Fire and Salt'. The porter held a finger to his lips to warn his visitor to be silent before the men guarding the doors quietly opened them and ushered the Herald and his escorts inside. Inside the men carefully made their way to one side of the circular chamber, the Priestess was already well into her routine.

The scent of scorched bay leaves and salt permeated the air in the room, and flickering lanterns placed in a circle about the Priestess cast dancing silhouettes on the dark walls. Inside the circle of lamps another circle had been traced. It was made of ash and red clay, powdered eggshell and sulfur, drawn with exact and reverent care by Priestess Urha Kane herself.

The Priestess knelt before it, her garments a fusion of silk and hide and adorned with charms that clicked softly when she moved. Her dark skin gleamed with oil and sweat; her forehead marked with a glyph in chalky white. Her eyes—dark as pitch and just as unreadable—rested on the six people who had come before her willingly.

They sat arrayed in a half-moon of silence, each on a velvet cushion. The young man with the shaking hands. The woman who clutched her locket like a crucifix. The elderly banker whose daughter had been missing since spring. All had come not for spectacle, but for the thing that came after—*hope.*

The people gathered before the Priestess did not seek an audience with the dead, but confirmation that someone lost still lived. They sought evidence that the resources consumed in seeking their missing loved ones hadn't been squandered. That the weeks, months or years spent waiting were not in vain.

And to this end, each brought with them some treasure from their past as required by the Priestess. A token that bound them to the person they sought. A bright ribbon for a woman's hair. A small, children's bible. A single, red rose pressed flat and brittle. These items now lay at the center of Urha's craft, within the inner circle.

"You seek light in darkness," Urha said, her deep voice strangely soothing. "A sure step on uneven footing. Are you prepared to receive that which you seek?"

By differing degrees of hesitation, the supplicants affirmed their wishes. Urha accepted this with a solemn nod, then she grew still.

The Priestess burst into rapid, choppy movements and words from some unknown language began spilling from her lips. The strange intonations were broken periodically by prayers or pleas formed of English as the priestess called on the spirits to bring her word on the missing loved ones.

In the Chamber of Still Waters the atmosphere was much more serene. Still warm, still dim with tiles of dark stone that seemed to absorb more light than they reflected. A shallow black pool dominated the center of this room. Perfectly calm and ringed with glowing, lotus-shaped lamps, each flickering with a faint violet flame. The scent of rose water and burned myrrh lingered in the air like a dim memory.

Asha Manna, the Eye of Kashmir, waited barefoot upon a large, flat stone. She stood elegant and still, already deep into her trance. Clad in a sari of dark indigo trimmed in gold thread, her hair coiled atop her head like a crown of dusk, exposing her graceful neck and framing her beautiful, serene face. Her eyelids, dusted with copper, glowed in the soft light of the lotus lamps.

Her long fingers moved in mudra over the pool's surface, but they did not touch. Her three petitioners knelt on silk cushions at an appropriate distance due to the diviner's station. All things must be in their proper place, and time, for the Eye of Kashmir to open.

Asha opened her eyes and beheld the three people.

The first was a widow, whisper-thin and brittle, her bracelets hung loose on her withered arms. One, a publisher with shaky, ink-stained fingers and deep-set eyes. The last was a young woman, no older than twenty, clutched a diary bound in soft leather so tightly the cover bore impressions of her fingers. Like all the chambers, seating for an audience was arrayed along two walls. All the chairs were filled.

"Welcome seekers," The Eye of Kashmir intoned in her strong, but melodic voice.

It was not the volume of Asha Manna's voice that startled Katia awake. It was only that these were the first words spoken since they had taken their seats along the dark wall.

Katia meant no disrespect to her peer, but the dim room had been so warm and quiet, and Katia rarely slept anymore, generally catching brief moments of respite like now. The startled woman froze; afraid she had interrupted the séance with her waking.

The Eye continued speaking in her soothing voice and Kat allowed herself to relax—a bit. Neither her uncle nor cousin, one at each side, made any reaction, and she relaxed more. As her heart rate slowed, she rubbed her eyes beneath the dark spectacles feeling sand beneath her eyelids. Tension remained in her chest like an aggressive corset, but she was used to that by now.

Katia had been living with the knowledge that one day, any day—even today, she could lose her mind. It had been five years since she first heard the voices, if that's what they were. Not really speaking. It was confusing.

They felt like voices. She could sense intent behind the sounds. As if they had direction or agency of their own. A purpose. And Kat feared that it was a very dark purpose.

Sounds like a thousand fists pounding the earth, or maybe ten thousand. A rhythmic tattoo at the back of her mind, always. Raging out of control at times, and in those moments the hammering in her mind became distorted and words emerged. Not words she could understand, always just too quiet, or too warped to be deciphered. But they carried emotion with them. She could not comprehend the angry words; but she could feel the perturbation behind them. Fear, lust, greed, hate. Katia was intimate with every possible state of mind by this time. It didn't take the young woman long to realize that she was sensing the emotions of those around her.

When she had finally confided in her family, her uncle Gallo, a devotee of the spiritualist movement, saw the potential in her 'gift'. Her uncle also wisely identified an opportunity to give purpose to her suffering and support their entire family spread across two continents. And his plan had been wildly successful; The Angel of Vengeance was known throughout the world.

Despite her success, the thundering in her mind was always there, an unrelenting violation. Demanding her constant attention and eroding her focus, wearing her thin over time. Like some sinister machine it had slowly ground her defenses down over the few short years it plagued her. A constant reminder: *soon it will all end.*

The young woman could not imagine how it worked; but she did understand the ramifications of her decline. One day she would no longer be strong enough to hold the walls up, and they would crash down around her. And everyone near her. One day she would end up in a filthy, stained room at an asylum like the old woman who had boarded at her house when she was a child.

Kat was very young, and her parents didn't speak of it much, even today. But the young woman had heard enough stories of morose sanatoriums and the condemned souls therein to be fearful of her own future. Would she know? Would she still hurt? Or would the madness drive all sense and reason from her mind completely?

She pushed the thoughts away as she had done countless times before. At the end of the day, it didn't matter. All she had ever wanted, since they had been children, was to be with William Kelly. But that future was gone. Why? Because two things in this life were certain in Kat's opinion: first, she was going to lose her mind; and second, she would never do anything to harm or burden Will. How could she ever make him understand the machine?

Kat pushed her dark thoughts deep down, then chided herself for her pride. Her suffering was no more or less than so many others. No worse than the old widow they had laughed and joked about after the men came for her. Now Kat understood why her parents had been so solemn, had chastised them for their off-color remarks. There were times, alone in the dark, when she wondered if her callous treatment of the old woman had somehow invited the madness.

But the madness brought something else, something that seemed to investigate the minds of others, imparting that information to Kat. She didn't understand how or why, nor did she want to. It was every bit as terrifying as the rest of her madness, but it did offer her a skill that was in demand. One that perhaps she could use to help her family...before she became only a burden upon them.

Katia focused on her breathing, pushing down the fear. Pushing out the sounds around her that bent themselves into secrets and remarks about the others around her. It had taken practice to ignore the voices, a lot of practice. Particularly when they are talking about her family—or Will. She assumed all the noise regarding them were lies, she had to. Anything else would promptly drive her mad.

Kat focused on the Eye of Kashmir, and her soft voice. And not sleeping.

Chapter 6

Will finally reached the 35th floor. The crowds thinned enough somewhere in the early twenties, but by then he'd had his day's workout. Right out of the lift he was back in a crowd of odd people. These floors were referred to as the mid-tower, sandwiched between the dusky lower floors of the building's base, and the gilded penthouses known as the psychomanteum.

Fischer had opened the rooms in the building to mediums and occultists. Giving them free room and board so long as they practiced their arts out of these rooms. Will had no legitimate reason to access the files on the Eventide Investigation, so he had to rely on hearsay. This fact left gaps in his understanding of the ongoing inquiries, he did turn up the name of the Pinkerton agent living in the building and had arranged a meeting with the man.

The bootleggers had provided him access to the mid-tower, and the Pinkertons would unknowingly provide Will access to the psychomanteum. He would pay for all of this, of course. The Agency would make certain he never worked in their industry again, or law enforcement in general. And Mary wasn't the only personal acquaintance that Will had played loose with the truth about his intentions. But he believed Kat was in danger, and so all other concerns fell by the wayside. Carla slipping her police chaperon the same day that Kat arrived in New York was too much of a coincidence to be ignored.

As Will weaved his way through the crowd in the hallway, knots of people collected near doorways forming choke points in his path. He stood waiting for the crowd to thin, a name on the placard to his right held a familiar name, Darcy Hoyt. A name he'd heard Mary mention more than once. This place, the mid-tower, was where Mary normally spent her evenings at the Eventide.

Will had never been here before, why would he? These people pandered snake oil and empty promises to the bored at best and the desperate at worst. Which is fine if you're an heiress like Mary O'Shea, but Will has seen too many widows or lost families break their finances chasing after the vague promises from people like this. Thus, Mary's surprise when he had imposed himself on her to join her this night at The Eventide.

And it was ostensibly the reason for Kat breaking their engagement, his disfavor for her occupation as a spiritualist. But Will knew better. They had known each other since they were children, she couldn't lie to him any more than he could lie to her. And while that sounded like a person deluding oneself, Will's line of thinking always ended at the same conclusion: he knew Kat. Knew who she really was, fierce, loyal and honest. But she did have one weakness: her family.

That led Will's detective mind to the most likely explanation for what was happening to the woman he intended to marry. Her uncle, newly arrived from the Old Country, used his connections in polite society to leverage or buy information about people. He passed this information to his nephew, who then fed the information to Katia. The old man had no direct contact, and Katia would do anything to help her family. And another fraud was born.

He did not blame Kat; she was using the information given to expose criminal behavior and that would justify her actions to herself. No, Will placed the blame directly on her family, where it belonged. That her family had directly interfered with their relationship, he could not say for certain. But knowing Kat and accepting that she was still the woman he loved, he could only deduce that she was trying to protect him. From what, he had no idea.

Will turned his mind back to his job, finding the shadow agent. He had been surprised to learn Pinkerton had any agents this deep in Eventide. Will guessed the agency was investigating the fraud committed against the most vulnerable in society. Perhaps the number of lives affected by the actions of these people had finally reached a threshold that prompted the authorities to employ the Pinkertons to investigate. Or maybe it wasn't how many have been affected, but who specifically had been swindled. Fischer was swimming with sharks.

And if he was actively stealing from his clientele or their families? Will had seen more than one case of a 'mind reader' who took what information they could worm out of a client and then used it to blackmail other parties involved. Or even the client. Thus, spreading the ruin such people inflicted over an even wider area. But also increasing the danger to Fischer himself.

Offering so many people free room and board required deep resources. So where was Fischer getting his? The man had never been that wealthy. Rumor had also informed Will that several children of the city's wealthy elite had moved into The Eventide, permanently, handing over their vast fortunes to the tower's builder. If true, then one way or another, Andrei Fischer's days would soon be running out.

The fact that the Pinkertons saw fit to use what is known as a 'shadow agent' confirmed one of the other bits of gossip; that the Agency had failed to get a man into the psychomanteum. Shadow agents work outside of the Agency, and as such have more freedoms, but also often require more resources to put into place than a bellboy or a porter. That is always the first point of infiltration, on the inside, as an employee.

Getting an agent to infiltrate as a spectator is simple, of course, that just takes money or power or dropping the right name. But the Pinkertons were unable to get an asset employed in the highest part of the building, the psychomanteum. Not because the agents vanished or turned up floating in the bay. But after the agents were hired, they each promptly sent word by messenger, resigning from the Pinkerton Agency, and even leaving their families.

Will had never heard of such an occurrence and doubted the veracity of the claims. Likely one or two operatives had made the move from law to crime, and the resulting shock had born a scandalous tale that echoed only a passing resemblance to reality. The entire scenario sounded silly, to be honest. In his mind he always imagined the last line of the tale as if it were one of the spiritualist's ghost stories: *and they have never left the building since.*

Silly or not, he didn't trust anyone working in this building. That included the Agency's shadow agent. Not that he necessarily had anything against the man, but he certainly had nothing for him. Oh, except for the package, he thought idly.

As Will passed through yet another dense pack of humanity, he spotted an a-frame sign that bore three concentric circles, like a bullseye, but colored only in shades of blue. Over that was stamped the name 'Professor Lucien Virelli, Mesmerist'. The man in the doorway, however, gave him pause. Correction; Will had a lot against this shadow agent.

Leaning casually against his door jam, the man met Will's eyes. He wore a finely tailored, deep brown three-piece suit that featured a subtle crosshatch texture, causing the fabric that caught the light just right to reflect its fine quality. A dark tie, knotted to precision, stood out crisply against the white shirt collar. Hair was freshly trimmed, and his squared jawline was dusted with a meticulously trimmed beard.

George Arthur Wence. A former agent, or so Will had thought, disgraced for accepting bribes from one of the factory owners he was investigating. Wence had expensive tastes and wasn't choosy how he came upon the means to feed those sensitivities. Will was disappointed with the Pinkertons; George Arther Wence should be in jail, not operating under even less supervision. The shadow agent recognized Will in return.

"Why, William Kelly," Wence said in a smooth baritone, "as I live and breathe."

"Professor," Will replied with a nod, making his way into the man's apartment.

The man's room was neat and clean, like its owner. Doors flanked Will on all sides. A large, unadorned table stood at the center of the room surrounded by chairs. Will supposed Wence didn't need all the trappings of a medium, his power was his mind, not his spirits. And Wence had a cunning mind.

On the table was a Boston bag, its sturdy, cowhide leather, in pristine condition like everything in Wence's care, open just far enough to expose the crimson uniform Will would need to enter the upper tower.

Will handed off the package he'd carried from the lobby, which

GEORGE WENCE

Wence accepted with a wry smile.

"Oh, William, you shouldn't have."

"I didn't," Will replied, returning his attention to the leather bag. "Luther Fuller wrapped that just for me."

Wence curled his lip in disgust, opened the door to his room and tossed the gift into the hall. Will smiled at the man's reaction, he didn't blame him. He reached into the bag and drew out a crimson uniform with matching cap and a map.

Will held up the map, a question on his face.

"That's your way in," the shadow agent explained. "With everything going on here tonight, the Angel and all, they don't have enough men to guard all the access points. This post will be vacant until the crowds thin."

"Thoughtful of you."

Neither man would question the other about his purpose or duties. There was no trust between them, an unspoken agreement between professionals. Will certainly would not be following the dubious plan concocted by Wence. He now had a pretty good idea why the Agency had failed to penetrate the high tower of Eventide, and it was Wence.

The mesmerist flipped open an ornate wooden box that sat on the table and drew out a cigarette. He lit it with a match and regarded Will through a smoky cloud.

"You'd better hurry," Wence commented.

"Yes," Will agreed as he donned the jacket and hat, he would deal with Wence later.

Map in hand, Will opened the door and turned to Wence. A smile and a tip of his hat to the shadow agent, then he moved quickly toward the elevators. Once out of Wence's sight, Will put his own plan into action. He sought out a small group of people waiting for an opening among the mediums. Will leaned in and spoke quietly to a gentleman, handing him the map Wence had provided. Will set a convenient distraction in motion thanks to Wence's dubious labors.

"Now keep this quiet, as only a few are allowed entry to the private reading." He paused once, turning back to the man, he held a finger to his lips, then carried on down the hallway.

Will took the first elevator that arrived. Now he needed to reach the elevators on the mezzanine that would grant access to the psychomanteum.

"This car going up," the porter said as the doors opened.

Will stepped into the car.

"This car is going down," the detective corrected.

The man opened his mouth to protest but then closed it at the sight of the crimson uniform.

* * *

Carla listened to the old woman drone on about someone's lost loved one, or pet, she couldn't be sure. The need to quell her vengeance ratcheted up her discomfort, causing her to squirm and fidget in her chair along the dark wall of the room. She had entertained the idea of just walking out, but three men stood before the door, two of them in the red livery that, to Carla, represented authority, and so she abandoned the idea.

Instead, she squirmed on the too-padded chair and generally disturbed those around her. She ignored their stares and mumbled recriminations, lost in the grinding obsession that drowned out all rational thought. Carla understood she was not supposed to leave, none of them were, until the Priestess had finished her séance. But still she struggled to conjure up some reason to slip from the room.

So, when she noticed the three men turn and open the doors to leave Carla shot out of her seat like a coiled spring. The slim woman slipped between two of the men and was in the hallway before any of them realized it. The doors shut with a soft click and only then did the escort realize what had happened.

"Ma'am," a man in crimson said politely, "we ask that you remain in the room until the session is over."

"You don't understand," Carla explained desperately, "I must go…"

"Alright," he raised a hand to still her argument. Misreading the situation, he turned to his companion and spoke, "I will see the Herald to the Queen, you escort the lady to the powder room, then see her back to the séance."

The man nodded and took Carla by the elbow. The fiery woman nearly clawed the man's face but calmed when she realized the number of men in her way had reduced from five down to one. She racked her brain for a plan as they turned a corner, now out of sight of the men. But nothing came.

She had the gun, but the sound would bring more men than she had cartridges, and she would never reach Katia. Then there was the ring, but she considered that a last resort, perhaps for herself if the need arose. Besides, the scarlet uniform featured a high collar, and his hands were gloved, such an attack could easily fail. And if it did? She had no hope of overpowering the man.

Panic began to set in beneath the dark veil, and so she did nothing. Only allowed herself to be guided until they reached a velvet-wrapped alcove like so many others they had passed. But this one was different. Inside on the right was an open doorway, a heady mix of perfume, cosmetics, and faint cigarette smoke drifted out. The man nodded, then turned his back on the alcove and stood guard in the hallway.

Like many ladies' powder rooms, it was less restroom and more of a plush sanctuary, designed for lingering rather than rushing. The walls were alternately clad in pale silk damasks and lacquered panels that gleamed under the soft golden glow of shaded sconces. Along one side, a row of ornate gilt-framed mirrors stretched the length of a marble-topped vanity. Each of the mirrors was flanked by globe lights in frosted glass that cast a soft, flattering radiance on freshly powdered cheeks and painted lips. A silver tray sat before each mirror, and neat rows of crystal perfume bottles, cut-glass dishes of hairpins and face powder all sat within easy reach.

Carla passed the velvet-cushioned stools and dainty upholstered chairs that provided seating for the mirrors. The plush burgundy carpet muffled the sound of her footsteps. She confirmed no attendant was on station, and a few moments later Carla had confirmed the room was empty but for herself. She stopped for a glance in one of the mirrors, but something about her reflection seemed wrong, she didn't recognize herself. She ripped her gaze away from the disturbing visage.

She felt a flood of emotions building in her chest as she failed to think of any answer. She considered trying to brain the man with the butt of the pistol, but it was a small weapon, and she was not very strong. She cast an appraising eye over the delicate chairs and stools, and while she was no expert, she didn't believe any of the furniture would be sturdy enough to harm the man. She put her head in her hands in frustration.

Carla breathed deep several times before letting her gloved hands slide down her face, and that's when she saw it. Whether it was the distorted reflection or some macabre inspiration within her, her gaze lit upon the mother-of-pearl knobs of her hatpins. The old warning: never fall asleep with your hat on rattled around her demented mind. One hand rose absently as she watched in the mirror, and drew out the long, metal pin.

But her madness only extended so far. Could she kill another human. Yes, she had determined this already, and anyone who stood between Carla and the justice she deserved was her adversary. What she did doubt was the likelihood the pin would be able to pierce the man's jacket. She would only be able to strike once; she had to kill him with one blow, so it must be the heart.

Or the head.

Carla thought again of the cautionary tale of the hatpins and

UPPER TOWER USHER

lying down. Her eyes were drawn to the crystal and glass on the silver tray. An idea took form, weak at first, but the more she rolled it over in her mind the more confident she became. She would still only have one shot, so she removed the pistol from her purse and secreted it on her person among the folds of dark silk. If that didn't work, she would use the ring.

The woman made her way out of the powder room. The plush carpet concealed any sound of her approach. The man glanced down when he noticed a crystal cylinder roll out from between his feet. When he did so, the back of his neck was exposed above the uniform's stiff collar.

Carla struck hard with the hatpin, mustering every bit of force she could. The metal spine slid into the man's neck and skewered his brain. Driven by madness and fear, her strength drove the hatpin out the top of his skull with a wet pop, a sound that made her knees weak. The guard collapsed and Carla snatched at his coat and pulled with all her strength to direct his fall backwards.

The dead man fell on top of Carla pinning her to the thick carpet, and she fought a sudden bout of claustrophobia as she struggled to free herself. Once free, she attempted to drag the body further into the alcove. She intended to conceal her crime more effectively, but her eyes began to water, and a burning sensation bloomed deep in her throat. A chemical taste formed in her mouth, and the burning in her eyes and throat intensified.

The guard's hat tumbled off his head, revealing more than just the exit wound from her hatpin. Around the silver tip of the pin, something bubbled and hissed. Confused and convinced that the strange malady originated from the corpse, she instinctively recoiled from touching it further. Abandoning the task of concealing her crime, and driven by self-preservation, she stumbled out into hallway and felt her way along one wall as she wiped at her burning eyes.

Carla stopped moving until she could see again, she didn't want to stumble blindly back to the room without her escort. When her vision cleared her heart began to slow a bit. She realized she had left both the hatpin and her purse behind, but couldn't muster the courage to go back for either. So she mourned their loss and turned away continuing the search for her prey.

Chapter 7

The Herald passed through the doorway into another world. The Observation room was a refuge from the light and noise of the mid-tower and the Room of Salt and Fire. He was grateful for the peace he found there. The tour had been a remarkable event of new sights and sounds, new sensations and experiences. And it had all proved as overwhelming for the Herald as it was novel.

The room was warm and dark; a vast circular chamber that's breadth was cloaked in shadow so thick it felt like being swathed in lush velvet. The air was still, and a soft quiet lay over all within, broken only by the faint voice of a woman that was piped into the room somehow. A thick carpet swallowed the sound of his footsteps. Overhead, the domed ceiling glowed with soft gold leaf before rising away into shadow. The dark walls were paneled in some rare wood that shimmered subtly when it cast back the soft glow of the sconces arranged around the chamber's perimeter.

Set into the far wall, a great black oval dominated the room and drew focus like gravity. It stretched nearly from floor to ceiling just as it did in the summoning room. Through the great mirror's smooth surface, the Herald could see Babi Ester as she held court for her petitioners. That explained the voice he was hearing.

Queen Carlotta stood before the great speculum, she turned when the Herald entered the room, dismissing his escort with a nod.

"It's remarkable," said the Herald, "all of it."

"Yes," the Queen replied. She didn't turn to face him, her focus seemed strangely divided, "yes, it is."

"The Eventide is a marvel of scientific genius," he stepped closer to the mirror.

"I cannot take credit for the building," she replied, one hand absently gestured behind him, "That was Fischer, while he lived."

The Herald turned as a flash of light erupted nearby, illuminating a man sitting in an overstuffed chair. Andrei Fischer's tall form was folded into the smoking chair, the light from the match revealed his neat, silver hair, combed back from a high forehead. He smiled and nodded to the Herald as he applied the match to a tobacco pipe. A full, well-groomed mustache gave him a calm, dignified appearance. His tanned and weathered skin, marked with fine lines, spoke of both age and experience.

The architect stood, tossing the spent match into an ashtray, and stopped to admire the mirror. Or perhaps it was his reflection he sought. Fischer fussed with his finely tailored dark suit and the smooth brown tie he wore over the crisp white shirt. A pale folded handkerchief and fountain pen peeked out from his breast pocket, small but deliberate touches of sophistication.

"I take no credit," the man replied smoothly, his lips twisted in a wry smile. "The architect built all of this to delight his wife. He hoped his invention might amplify her powers of spiritualism."

There was a long silence before Carlotta noticed. She turned

ANDREI FISCHER

her attention away from the scene in the next room and focused it on the Herald. She deduced his discomfort.

"The Herald may speak freely in the presence of the Emissary." She turned her attention back to Babi Ester.

The man spoke, hesitantly at first, but seemed to draw comfort as he progressed through what was obviously a rehearsed speech.

"No one wishes to diminish your many, and illustrious accomplishments; however, some of our people do have concerns about the safety of the process you have developed. Most especially those concerns related to the long-term effects of the process on our people and our home."

"Diminishing me is precisely what you seek." She replied, not looking at the man.

"My Queen, the council does not seek the cessation of your efforts," he said delicately, "they simply wish for you to reduce the output...at least for a short time."

She still didn't look at the Herald.

"There is too much power for our batteries to contain, we will soon reach a critical point." He pleaded with her. "There's too much power."

"Too much power," she repeated, now looking him in the eyes, her head cocked in a decidedly human fashion. "Too much power? Too much sustenance? Too much security?"

She shook her head and looked away. "You, none of you, truly understand the danger of losing this power. And you should.

Build better batteries."

"We are, but our technology has its limits," the Herald explained. "Time is what we need, and we cannot manufacture that."

A long silence followed, broken only by Babi Ester's distant voice and Fischer drawing on his pipe.

"Do you remember the way things were? Before the surplus?" She shook her head, "no, of course you don't. You are young, you forget we used to hunt for the shimmering globes that tied our worlds together, harvesting what little energy we could glean from them before they faded.

How we became dependent upon those short-lived wells for nourishment at first, and then our advancement as a society became hopelessly entwined with them. Without the power they provide…" she turned to look at him, "billions will perish."

The Herald was young, but he had heard the stories. All of their kind knew the stories. Tales of war and famine. Tales of vast death and destruction as his species strived for control over the meager resources provided by the glowing orbs of energy.

Carlotta turned away again, but she was not done speaking.

"Now for the first time, we have a surplus, and we must maintain that surplus." She seemed to grow distant again. "I don't know what they taught you before sending you here, but the human world changes quickly. One day they will move on from this place, or this construction will fall around us."

Fischer tapped his pipe on an ashtray.

"Either way, this source of power is finite, if not in quantity, surely in time."

"You do not fear the humans?" He was surprised.

The Queen locked him in a fierce glare. "I do not fear that which I can manipulate."

"You fear the humans?" Fischer asked the man.

"Of course I fear the humans," the Herald stated, "they have constructed a tower that pierces our universe. They discharge lethal amounts of energy, and do not even realize it. Why do you not fear them?"

"Because" the old man said as he sat back down in the large chair, "they are harmless."

"Oh? How long will it be before they build another of these... Eventide's, or a hundred? How long before they use those towers to invade our world? What would we do? How would we fight them? They are giants.

And what will we do when we cannot use or store all the power you are harvesting from the humans? And it is a matter of when, not if. As I have said, our storage devices are nearly over-capacity. What then?"

The Herald leaned in to drive his point home.

"What if they discover what you are doing?"

The last question was met with silence, though whether it was brought about by contemplation or contempt he couldn't be sure.

"Don't think they'd understand what they found," Fischer said, he blew air through the pipe to clear the bowl, "that's the point, this place will be gone before any human realizes what they built. Even Fischer himself never realized the full scope of his accomplishment before his death. No reason to believe the others will be any different."

"You say that continuing this process might cause a disaster in our world," the Queen added, "I tell you this process will end when the humans end it, and that will be a disaster in our world."

"The best we can do is get all of the energy we can before the gateway closes." Fischer struck a match.

"But if we cannot contain what we have taken…it won't matter when it closes." The Herald stepped to the mirror to face the Queen. "What you have done is open a deluge into our world that we cannot consume nor store fast enough. We will reach a breaking point, and soon. You cannot be so naïve as this I'Pa."

He realized his mistake instantly, but there was no way to take it back. Carlotta's head tilted to one side as she regarded him for a moment, then she lifted a hand near the man's ear and slammed the Herald's skull against the mirror with enough force to make it ring like a gong. This elicited gasps and a brief shriek from the other side of the glass, and a low chuckle from Fischer.

The Herald had been caught off guard by both the Queen's strength and intent. The impact caused him to nearly detach from the human's brain. That would have been a death sentence; his escorts had informed him that the host body he was in was scheduled for destruction. This meant the human was effectively dead and an Outsider would have to keep the autonomic systems of the body running.

However, if this process was interrupted, the human would die, and the Herald lacked both the training and the skill to operate a corpse. That would leave him trapped in the human's skull. A long, slow death. But that was the least of his problems; he could feel her now.

Disconnected from the host's senses, he was left to his native senses. Humans were basically very tall bags of liquid attached to a rigid frame. As such, they conducted vibrations very well. So, when two humans touched, even though the host body generated a lot of noise itself, the Outsiders could communicate in their native fashion. Vibration.

He now understood why his masters feared I'Pa.

The Queen was enormous, several times the size of his own hive queen. As the vibrations increased, the Herald was able to better define her symmetry and was terrified. I'Pa was more than that, she was a genetic throwback. Her lines were slim and graceful, built for punching through hive walls and killing the drones within. Descended from warrior hives that relied on consuming other hives for sustenance and materials, I'Pa was a relic of bygone days. Yet here she was, controlling the most powerful alliance of hives their people had ever seen. The true scope of his masters' fears became painfully clear. Why hadn't they warned him?

"Never presume to speak to me informally, drone, I will not have it." The vibrations were soft, consoling, everything a drone needed it to be, he wanted to serve I'Pa. "I do not care what your masters fear, they are fools. I will run this operation the way it must be run, and if your job is to impede my efforts, or find a way to make my job more difficult, I will devour you whole and shit out your carapace and have it sent to your hive-mates. Am I understood?"

Her rage was an undertone in the oscillation that tickled his antennae and spread ripples of terror through his mind. He had addressed this Hive Queen as an equal, and now he was about to be eaten, something that wasn't supposed to happen in modern society, but that fact was cold comfort to him now.

I'Pa released the Herald who tumbled to the floor in a heap. The transition was difficult, especially for the uninitiated and unprepared. His human host remained stunned for several moments before he was able to reposition himself and resume control over his host. Slowly, much slower than before, the Herald regained control of his human. His trainers had warned him, and they had been right; riding a human was much more complicated than could be explained, it must be experienced.

When she saw the human's mouth moving mechanically, she knew the Herald could hear her again.

"We must pull as much energy from the humans as possible before this…Eventide comes to bore them, and they tear it down. This will happen, I have seen their impatience, and it will happen at the worst possible time for our people."

"You can tell your Council how this is going to happen, according to my will, not theirs." I'Pa lifted the Herald's face with a hand on his chin, staring directly in the human's eyes. "I will tease out the means by which the humans constructed this tower. And given time, I will be able to recreate these devices for our own people."

She released his chin and stood.

"You may also remind them that they lack any credible means of stopping me."

The Herald mumbled something unintelligible.

"What was that?" I'Pa leaned closer.

"Hive Killer," he managed.

The Queen recoiled in surprise. She had not considered that. Hive Killers were thermobaric weapons used to destroy entire hives. The benefit was massive destruction without spreading the fire along the connecting structures that linked all the hives. At one time catastrophic wars had led to a severe population decline in their species. Many of the hives destroyed were eliminated only due to their proximity to other warring hives.

This disaster led to improvements in directing and containing the destruction of future wars. Hence, the Hive Killer, a weapon that extinguished its own fire. And it was successful; wars were nearly unheard of in their modern age. I'Pa knew Hive Killers well, she had more of them than any other hive. More than many hives combined.

"Is that a threat?" Fischer asked, his voice edged dangerously, "your masters intend to risk open war with our alliance?"

"No," he cleared his throat as he slowly regained control of the human's body and struggled to his knees. "They have constructed a Hive Killer five hundred times more powerful than any built previously...to use on the humans."

I'Pa's eyes narrowed as she saw the threat, Dul'Sa did not see it, and from inside Andrei Fischer's body the Emissary pressed him.

"Five hundred times more powerful, well, used in the human world that should yield…"

"The destruction of a single building."

I'Pa and Dul'Sa shared a glance.

She would not be able to eat the Herald after all; he may need to be tortured for information.

Chapter 8

Babi Ester led the group out of the summoning chamber. Her duties fulfilled, the woman laughed and entertained her admirers as they made way for the Angel. Babi Ester had wanted to witness the young woman's performance but had been told the room was already full. She shook it off with good humor and turned her focus to her own fans.

Mary O'Shea sat at the leftmost edge of the long black table facing the medium. Her smile was tight as a seam under tension. She did not look up when the Angel entered the room, but her spine straightened at the sound of rustling fabric as she passed behind Mary.

Across from her, seated together was a middle-aged couple: the man round-shouldered and balding looking more than a bit defeated. The woman beside him was sharp-faced and draped in navy lace. She clutched a handkerchief that made regular forays beneath her short veil. The man's brother sat beside them; Mary had overheard that much of their conversation. Younger than his brother by several years and looking as though he'd rather be anywhere else.

Gallo escorted Katia to the great chair at the head of the table. Her seat faced outward, but her back now aligned perfectly with the oval of darkness the mirror formed behind her. A deliberate positioning, said to intensify the voices of the dead. Even draw them from the away from the void nearer to the world of the living.

The guests took their seats, some nervously fidgeting in their chairs for a bit, but all attention was inexorably drawn to the

BABI ESTER

medium before the mirror. As the crimson pages began to close the doors of the chamber, a voice called out. Female and foreign, muffled but still sharp-edged.

"—She will see me! You listen— She will see me!"

A man's voice responded, stern but calm, trying to pacify the enraged woman. More arguing ensued. The volume became muted, but the words lost none of their heat. Mary turned her head slightly toward the door, the event drawing the interest of those inside the room.

And then the doors clicked shut. Silence.

* * *

The heavy doors had barely closed before Carla Rios exploded.

"I said she would see me!" She shrieked, voice raw and scraping. Her arm flailed, landing a slap across the face of one of the scarlet attendants. An audible crack that drew more red clad men. "You heard me! I said—"

Two of the staff seized her arms, but Carla twisted in their grip like a feral animal. Her veil slipped off revealing her dark, wild eyes. Her lipstick had smudged into a twisted parody of a smile, and the weeping from whatever assaulted her eyes in the powder room left her with streaks of black tears.

"You have no idea what she did," Carla spat, eyes fevered. "You don't know who you're protecting—"

The men tried to calm her. One murmured softly to her in

French-accented English, the other tried to explain, "Miss, please, you are not on the schedule—"

"Schedule!" She snarled, her eyes went wilder, and she dug her nails into the wrist of one of the men. "Justice keeps no schedule!"

Then, with one hand free, Carla thrust it into her dress and pulled out the Pin-fire revolver, the vicious little antique shined in the light of the sconces. Her hand experienced a slight tremor, but she had practiced with the weapon. She knew how to use it.

Carla had just raised the gun when a tall, severe-looking man, dressed in the same red and black uniform as the others, appeared behind her. His gloved hand snapped forward with speed and grace Carla could never have expected. Carla gasped as her wrist was yanked forward, the revolver plucked cleanly from her grip and handed off to a nearby attendant before she'd even registered the pain.

"Son of a—" she tried to scream, but a firm hand was now clamped on her shoulder, and though he only squeezed lightly, her knees faltered all the same.

Her aggressor's features were sharp and symmetrical with smooth, pale skin and straight brows. He radiated authority. His clean-shaven face gave him an almost statuesque quality. His dark eyes were calm but unreadable, conveying a quiet intensity. The faintest suggestion of a frown hung at the corners of his mouth, as though neutrality was his default expression. The planes of his face were elegant in the form of bone architecture.

OS' FIL

Os'Fil, General of I'Pa's legions regarded the volatile female human with cold reproach. Carla quailed beneath his hard glare. She quickly looked away from his intense gaze and saw that the guards had snapped to attention, all eyes awaiting his command.

"Explain."

"She is mad," one of the men muttered, still gripping her other arm. "Tried to force her way into the séance."

"She's not on the schedule," the other man confirmed.

Os'Fil acknowledged his soldiers with a nod. His voice, when he spoke, was cool and low, yet easily understood.

"Take her." He ordered, and two of the four men accompanying him stepped forward to take Carla in hand.

Just as Carla had overcome her shock and was prepared to unleash another withering tirade, she was interrupted by another red-clad man who spoke to Os'Fil.

"General, humans are swarming the north-east stairwell, pushing our men back," he pulled out a folded paper and offered it to his commander. "And they brought Wence's map."

Os'Fil's jaw flexed when he looked at the paper. He didn't know what game Wence was playing, but the human would soon find out that the General did not play.

"Take what men you need," he ordered the man, "turn the humans back, and find the Pinkerton agent that Wence was supposed to aid. Bring him to me at once."

As the man departed, the General motioned to one of his escorts. "This agent may be more cunning than we anticipated," Os'Fil said, "make the rounds, alert the men to keep the vigil. He may try to use this as a distraction and enter by another means."

After his guard withdrew, Os'Fil looked down on Carla. He eyed her with a stare so flat and empty she felt like she was being assessed by an inhuman mind. He gave her the full measure of his attention now, watching her twitch.

"She's gone too far," he said at last. "And she's seen too much."

"She wants to see the Angel," supplied one of the men.

"Or kill her," offered another.

Os'Fil didn't reply. He raised his hand and two fingers flicked in a commanding arc.

"Bring her." Os'Fil turned toward the pages guarding the doors. "Back to your positions."

Two of the crimson men flanked Carla and lifted her by the arms. She shrieked again, kicked once, but they handled her efficiently, gently enough not to damage the woman—but they did not allow her to slow them down. They moved like men accustomed to handling reluctant human cargo.

As she was dragged kicking and struggling down the corridor, her shouts echoed off the marble. Os'Fil considered gagging her, but they were so near the Observation Room and all the rooms on the psychomanteum floors were sound-proofed, so he didn't bother.

Chapter 9

Will stepped out of the elevator on the ground floor. He decided he never wanted to ride another lift as long as he lived. But, since he was headed to the mezzanine elevators now, it was a commitment he would be unable to fulfill. He straightened his hat and coat and marched boldly up the steps.

At the sight of him, dusky-clad pages began to panic; this was not how the process was supposed to unfold. The scarlet pages should come down the elevator, not up the steps. Nevertheless, when he motioned for them to load the lifts with the next group of guests, they immediately complied.

Will joined the group in the car on the far left.

"Good evening, everyone," he offered his most charming smile. "Now, once we arrive on the floor, I will need all of you to move immediately to your right."

The people nodded their heads or quietly responded, accepting his instruction.

"And you can do all of us here at the Eventide a great service, if you would, by passing that instruction along to the people that will be exiting the other lifts."

More nods and acceptance.

"Fantastic," he smiled, "Welcome, I'm sure you all will have a memorable evening at the Eventide."

* * *

"Remarkable," Dul'Sa commented, preening his mustache. "I can feel her from here."

I'Pa nodded. "She is special."

"How many others, do you think?" Amazed, he bowed his head to the Queen, "of course, this means you have been right all along."

The Herald did not need any clarification concerning the subject of their discussion. Even he, on the other side of the room from the mirror could feel the Angel when she entered the chamber. The same power that had sustained his people for untold generations emanated from the human female in waves. It was remarkable. And it was terrifying.

How would the antenna react to this much energy? Surely this night, with this human, would fill all the batteries they had constructed to maximum. But he remained silent, sufficiently cowed by the Queen. The Herald began to fear his chances of surviving this mission were thin no matter how it turned out.

He watched as the young woman was helped to her seat by another human. How could a creature be so full of energy, and yet appear so weak and frail? His human eyes drifted to Queen Carlotta, and he considered how common she appeared among humans, but inside was a monster. Perhaps it was something akin to that.

Or more likely, his people still didn't understand the energy they relied on for existence. They did not truly understand the humans that produced that energy. But survival had driven them on at first; by now though, it had become gluttony. They began building larger and larger batteries to store the energy for later, not because they needed it, but because they could.

And the wiser among them had begun to question the lack of prudence involved in having so much of something they understood so little about. The Herald had argued on their behalf, his masters, not because he believed in their cause, but because it was his place. Now, in the human world, so far from his home and everything he knew, he began to see what the more cautious among them already saw. He understood the danger, but still, he remained silent.

He was drawn back to the conversation at the mirror when I'Pa turned and spoke.

The Queen pointed two fingers over his shoulder, "open the door."

It took the Herald a moment to process the instruction, mostly because he felt guilty, the aftereffects of having a hive queen in one's mind tended to linger for some time. But he rose quickly and made his way to the room's entrance. He had barely opened it when a tall, severe looking man in crimson entered. The man paused for a moment to scrutinize the Herald.

"The Herald," one of the other men behind him volunteered.

He dismissed the Herald from his mind with a nod and entered the room followed by a half dozen scarlet-clad porters, two of which were bearing a young human female. At least he took her for a human, she was screeching and struggling against the men, occasionally making wild threats that none of them understood.

"You filthy bastards!" She spat, kicking at one of the guards. "She murdered him! And you protect her?! You monsters!"

Carla's voice cracked on the final word, and she lapsed into silence.

"Os'Fil," the Queen greeted her General as a formality. She had felt his intentions, especially in this alien place, Os'Fil was a dependable rock she could always rely on.

"My Queen, this woman attempted to breach the summoning chamber. She became aggressive with the guard. And she produced this—"

At his gesture one of the guards held up Carla's pistol, the small antique revolver gleaming under the low light.

"I believe she intended to harm the Angel," Os'Fil finished.

"Carla Rios," she stated. I'Pa had studied everything she could find on the Angel, and there was a wealth of information about Carla Rios and the scandal.

Carla's head snapped up at her name.

"Oh, I know who you are. I know about the man you fell in love with, and the crime you helped him carry out." I'Pa turned her gaze back to the séance and Katia. "Neither of you were innocent."

"He was mine! We had a future!" Carla shrieked, twisting in the guards' grip. "She took all of that! You don't get to decide who receives justice!"

"Actually, as Queen, I do," I'Pa turned back to Os'Fil. "She's not to see the Angel. Not now. Not ever."

An animal scream tore from Carla's throat as she burst into furious action. She twisted away from her captors just long enough for one terrible moment. And in one frenzied lunge her hand snapped out. Something flashed in the light, a subtle glint of silver as she slapped Queen Carlotta across the throat.

I'Pa reeled back, more surprised than pained. She put a hand to her neck; her fingers found the welling blood from a tiny puncture just beneath her jawline. The guards regained control of Carla, wrenched her backward with more force than necessary. She shrieked in pain and collapsed to her knees. Through her tears and suffering, she laughed.

"Poison," I'Pa said calmly.

No one spoke. Os'Fil's face darkened; his Queen assassinated in his presence. The Herald stood now, slowly, unsure of what was happening, but the gravity of the situation was undeniable.

"Curare," Carla said in a now raw and hoarse voice, "a slow, painful death. It wasn't meant for you, all the same, it's your death now."

"She dosed the ring," I'Pa continued. Her fingers examined the wound with detachment. "Curare. I have heard of it."

"Do you need extraction?" Dul'Sa, wearing Andrei Fischer's corpse, stepped forward to examine the small red dot below Carlotta's chin.

"No." Her voice was cold, and the Queen's eyes did not leave Carla. "I can maintain the autonomic system manually. I will tire in time; and the damage done to Carlotta's body is catastrophic. This toxin will destroy the organs, and the body will decompose from the inside. I will need to find a new host soon."

Her fingers flexed, her breath became steady, but it cost her focus she would rather spend elsewhere. And the more the human body shut down, the more attention it would demand from her.

"How irritating." She frowned.

Carla watched as her world careened into something completely unrecognizable. Carlotta showed no sign of being affected by the poison. Had Carla done something wrong? Why was the woman not dying? Was the entire world against her? Carla began to breathe deep and heavy, rage building inside her.

The Herald could feel energy pulsing from the violent young human. It was not as intense as the Angel's emissions, but the Outsider gained a sliver of insight regarding the process by which humans generated the power that nourished his people. While he could not say why, the Herald was left with a dark, empty feeling.

I'Pa watched all of this passively. Carla was an unfortunate occurrence, but nothing more.

"Hand her over to the initiates. Let them train on something volatile for once." The Queen instructed Os'Fil, her tone reflected the dismissal of the woman. "Tell the authorities she escaped after attempting an assassination."

Carla jerked forward again violently, foam flecking her lips, but the guards held her fast. Deep in her throat she made a horrible sound, part cry and part scream.

"You cowards!" She screamed. "She's a murderer! You're all murderers—"

"Silence her," I'Pa commanded.

One of the guards obeyed without hesitation using the first item that came to hand. He brought down the pistol like a gavel at Carla's trial. The blow landed with a sound that immediately changed the atmosphere. A wet, splintering crack that silenced everything in the room, leaving only the faint words of the Angel to disturb the moment.

Carla crumpled at once. Like a puppet with its strings sheared through, she wound up in a tangled heap of twisted limbs. Her voice was replaced by a terrible stillness. No one moved to check on the girl. They didn't need to.

That silence said everything.

The shocked guard stared from the bloody gun, and then down to the motionless body, and back again.

"…Commander," he said after a moment. "I didn't mean—"

"You struck too hard," the general confirmed, his tone clinical. Not angry. Precise. The guard surrendered the weapon to Os'Fil, who instructed him. "You, dispose of its corpse in the incinerator."

The Queen commanded: "Tomorrow, inform the authorities the woman escaped. Hand over the pistol with the statement."

Os'Fil gave a curt nod and concealed the weapon inside his coat.

"And if they ask questions?" The Herald asked.

"They won't."

With a wave of her hand, I'Pa dismissed the man. The guard began dragging Carla's corpse toward the door leaving a darker smear on the thick burgundy. The Queen did not notice, she had already returned to the mirror. The Angel, Katia.

That strange flickering energy pulsing around her now like storm clouds. I'Pa thought of what she had learned from the humans; both from speaking to and observing these beings, she had easily manipulated them. But she was troubled by one fact; so many of the concepts she witnessed bore no parallel to anything in her world. This left her without any true context to understand them.

Chief among these was...*hope*. Humans believed in it. So much that one of them had built a tower that pierced two worlds; all in the vain *hope* it would make his mate happy. And it might have worked. Before her death, Carlotta had spoken highly of her husband. Even when she realized he had unintentionally killed them both.

Hope drew hundreds of humans to the Eventide daily where they traded their wealth to liars and swindlers for even more *hope.* Their eternal quest for this elusive and likely mythical salve had enabled I'Pa's race to thrive. She had always believed that hope had been key in the construction of the human concept of predestination, or at the very least formed the foundation upon which its tenets rest.

But what if she was wrong?

Katia Santoro was something else entirely. Her power dwarfed all those who had come before in I'Pa's memory. And it was not born of hope. The Queen had only brushed past the Angel briefly, but she sensed pain from the human...and no hope. Katia Santoro proved everything the Queen and her people believed about the humans was wrong.

Oh, certainly I'Pa had espoused her convictions that somewhere, a human with true gifts must exist. But honestly, such a stance had only been taken to buttress the argument in favor of continued harvesting. It was one more testimony added to the growing list of evidence aimed at convincing the other hive queens to see things her way. To continue gathering energy from humans.

And yes, empowering herself and her hive in the process. I'Pa had not and would not deny such a claim. In fact she was proud of her hive, her allies, her people. But she did not discriminate against her own kind. And she allowed the energy to flow to all. I'Pa wanted more hives in her alliance, not fewer.

When alive, Carlotta had believed predetermination occurred when someone was either fully selfless or consumed in selfishness. The human felt the universe somehow balanced all outstanding accounts. I'Pa felt that her efforts on behalf of her race qualified as selfless enough. Could there be a design for her?

It sounded mad, but so did a human that could mysteriously interpret the thoughts of other humans without obvious communication. Yet here I'Pa was, watching just such a human on the other side of the mirror. Right now. What else might Carlotta have been right about?

Destiny?

Maybe it wasn't just chance that brought the Angel here, tonight. Perhaps I'Pa was always meant to take her as host now. Oh, she had fully intended to do so, but later, after learning the secret of this human's power. She had hoped to preserve Carlotta, the face of the Eventide, for future use, but Carla's poison had rendered that plan moot. As long as Dul'Sa could ride Fischer's body, the ruse could continue.

"…Bring me the crown."

"You intend to take a new host with it?" Dul'Sa asked.

"Down here?" Os'Fil sought confirmation, hoping his queen would change her mind and enact the transfer in the tower, where it was much safer, and more discrete.

"I see no reason to wait," she said, "not anymore."

* * *

The room had settled into a respectful silence the way only a sacred place can. Katia Santoro, The Angel of Vengeance, sat in the chair at the head of the black-lacquered table. Its high back rose behind her like a judge's seat. A series of bent wooden slats formed the chair's back, framing the darkly garbed medium with dusky wings. This allowed the medium to remain cool, and unbeknownst to all in the room, also allowed those behind the mirror a clear view of the person in the grand chair.

The chair's exotic design made the seated person more visible to the spectators behind the mirror; however, it also made the one seated very uncomfortable. And so, Kat could not lean back and withdraw as she would have liked. She felt the expectations of the group as their eyes settled on her.

The smoky glass of the mirror reflected a muted replication of the room by design. More mystery, more unknown shadows or glimpses from the corner of the eye to fuel the psychic carnival. She rested her hands on the slick surface of the table, her gloved fingers splayed and motionless. The Angel mentally prepared herself for the coming storm.

Kat dipped her head forward to peer over the rims of her lenses and let the sound of the machine swell. Small, dark orbs peered out over larger glass orbs. The rhythmic pounding grew immediately, and a wave of random emotions washed over her. Panic rose unbidden at the violence of it.

She had prepared herself for this part, as always. Through practiced force of will she pushed back against the feelings until they reached a manageable intensity. Then she set about sorting the emotions by the people who radiated them. To her immediate left was her uncle, and her cousin sat at her right hand.

Katia passed over those whose emotions fawned over her 'gift' or those who radiated little emotion at all. Many who attended these events did so perfunctorily as befit their social standing and held little or no personal interest in spiritualism. And there were several of these people at her table tonight. Kat became concerned she might not be able to create the drama her hosts were hoping for.

Her attention was drawn to a redhead seated further down the table on her left side. She was wrapped in envy, only without the usual fawning, and held an intense curiosity. The woman looked familiar, but with the city's elite gathered here, it was likely that Kat had seen her face in a magazine or newspaper. She moved on around the table until she reached the other side on the opposite end from her.

Three people sat near each other, two men and a weeping woman. A middle-aged couple, passive, and well dressed. The man stroked the back of his wife's hand in a gentle, rhythmic fashion to console her. She muffled her grief in a thick, but feminine handkerchief. The man's brother completed the trio. Younger, overly stiff and radiating skepticism like armor against some dread danger.

The woman was tightly wound in navy lace, hands worked continuously, either dabbing her eyes and nose, or worrying the fabric of the personal cloth. Her eyes were haunted with something more than just grief. It wasn't sorrow that Katia detected rolling off the woman—it was guilt. It poured off her in waves, mingled with the maternal ache one would expect to find there.

Her husband hovered beside her, less composed than his wife, but far less haunted by their shared tragedy. His hands were trembling and his mouth worked at the corner. His eyes darted around periodically to the Angel and the others gathered around the table, but never at the mirror. He carried grief, but nothing more of interest to her.

The younger brother sat like a carved statue, his arms crossed before his chest in defense, mouth set defiantly. But Katia didn't need to see movement to feel what was inside him. Guilt and shame bled from every pore. Had his emotions manifested physically, they would have driven everyone from the room.

He barely glanced at her, or at anyone, but when he did, it was like he was issuing a challenge. There was something in his eyes. Not just defiance and not mourning. Something watchful. Measured. He was gambling.

The brother felt compelled to be here, she could sense this from the machine. His shame hit her like a physical blow. She hated shame most of all, likely because she felt so much of her own. Deserved or not, it didn't matter with her, but this man? The rhythmic drumming assured her that he had earned every single morsel of his shame.

They had come seeking answers of their son. Lost to them when he was just seven years old, drowned in the harbor last summer. Kat knew this from Enzo, who had overheard much of their conversation before the séance began. Most people handed over all the information someone needed to dissect their personal life in conversation with someone else, and then promptly forgot they had done so. It was little surprise that charlatans were so successful in the movement.

Katia tilted her head, ever so slightly as she pulled the threads of their emotion apart. This was her true gift, not speaking with the dead, or allowing spirits to speak through her. Never again. She would not call out to them again, ever. Oh, she had called out once—and something had answered her. But whatever it was, it was not a human spirit, and it had certainly *never* been a human. It had no interest in sharing knowledge, only in acquiring dominance over her.

Katia sat in silence at the head of the table, spine straight, gloved hands transferring her growing heat to the cold ebony. A small mercy: Kat always overheated in the séance. Her glasses sat low on her nose so she could see the family. Then she spoke.

"There is a boy here," this brought an immediate snuffle from the woman in her focus, but Kat had not caught his name. She cast her mind back to the newspaper in which she had read about his death. 'H', but that was the only clue she could remember, so she gambled, starting with the most common name first. "Henry?"

The explosion of emotion from the end of the table confirmed the accuracy of her guess. Kat's skin grew slick with sweat beneath the layers of dark clothing.

"He wants you to know that he is well," Kat relayed, "his passing was quick, and he felt no pain."

This brought fresh tears and a little hope, especially to the man. The woman, however, seemed ashamed of the contact. And the brother's fear spiked enough to slap Kat across her face. Now she was getting somewhere. She turned her full attention to the weeping woman.

Kat remembered a story about Henry the mother had told a reporter who interviewed the parents after the boy's death. It had stuck with her. "Henry would like to know if you remember when his grandmother died," She focused the machine on the boy's mother, "how you told him she was going to a better place, like the Bible says. But that he was concerned his grandmother wouldn't know how much he loved her."

The couple smiled at the memory, Henry's mother dabbing at her nose.

"And do you remember what you told your son?"

The mother smiled and nodded, whispering something only her husband could hear.

"You told him, that after someone dies, and they go to heaven, all secrets are revealed."

The impact was everything Kat had hoped for. Hope and love poured from the father. But the mother and the uncle had a very different response. While only the most observant person sitting in the dim room might have noticed the tight-lipped look that came over the uncle, or the stunned expression on the wife's face. Kat felt it all wash over her in a tidal wave of guilt and shame that made her sweat beneath the headdress.

The room fell into silence.

As Katia had expected, the uncomfortable silence was too much for the guilty. The husband noted his wife's curious response.

"Maggie?" He asked gently, "what's wrong, dear?"

The uncle stood abruptly, "this is all absurd."

"Lyle, sit down," the man's brother pleaded with him while trying to console his wife. The man complied with ill grace, his harsh gaze settling on the Angel.

"You are right to fear me," she told the younger man.

"I do not fear you," he spit, "I fear no woman."

Kat smiled wickedly. "You forget, Lyle, I speak with the dead. They share their secrets with me."

"Enough," the father put his foot down, "what is happening here."

She smiled at the man, "I am sorry, sir, but just as I am bound by my agreement with all of you around this table tonight; I am equally bound to honor all agreements made with the dead who contact me."

Everyone glanced at each other, confused, but not missing the gravity of the implication.

"I am bound to repeat Henry's words to you, regardless of the impact they might have." She smiled at the father again, trying to reassure him of something she had no control over. "Henry wants you to know that he loves you, very much, and had the utmost respect for you. He believes that your actions and behavior toward him would not have changed had you known the truth."

She turned to the mother.

"Henry is worried about you," this brought a whimper from the woman, "he is afraid that, because of your lies, you will not join him in heaven when you die."

The woman turned ashen, stunned.

"I don't understand any of—" the father started saying but was cut off by his brother.

"Shut up," Lyle growled at Katia, his feigned calm demeanor now irrevocably destroyed, "shut your mouth now, or I'll shut it for you."

Gallo and Enzo both stiffened at the threat. This was not a unique response, and the men had been forced to protect the Angel before now.

Kat just smiled thinly, "no, you won't, because you are a coward. Henry has a message for you too, Lyle."

Lyle made to rise, but his brother laid a restraining hand on his arm. The grip was firm; his brother was not letting anyone leave until he had some answers.

"Henry has a message for his real father."

The woman choked on a sob, her husband let his hand fall away, forgotten. Lyle turned several shades of red.

"He knows you didn't care. He knows you didn't even attend his funeral," another fact gleaned from the earlier gossip, the heinous nature of which caused it to lodge in her memory. "The death of your own son, acknowledged or not, and you passed on the opportunity to say goodbye."

Lyle maintained a disaffected look, but he squirmed in his seat.

"Henry wants me to assure you that he will always be watching you, Lyle. The way you never watched over him. Every day and every night. Every quiet moment you believe is your own. Every lie you live from now on—he will be with you. And he is waiting for you."

The Angel folded back into herself; in the dim light she seemed to melt into the giant, uncomfortable chair. The dark glasses were pushed back into position, blocking out the sight of the vengeance she had wrought. She was too hot and too tired to face it now.

Lyle had had enough. He stood, pointed at Kat, and worked his mouth for a moment. Then, thinking of nothing to say, turned on his heel and burst out of the room. The doors flung open, driving the porters away for their own safety. The husband wore a dark look, but helped his wife, now weeping even harder, up from the table and escorted her out of the room.

There was silence in the aftermath. A polite cough.

Then Queen Carlotta appeared in the doorway, and Katia had a very bad feeling.

"Everyone," Carlotta spread her hands wide to encompass them all, "I'm afraid that will be the Angel's final performance tonight. But fear not, this is but the first of many such engagements for The Angel of Vengeance at The Eventide."

Gallo and Enzo exchanged a confused look, and Katia's worry deepened. The Queen was not like other people. Up close, the machine had no response to her mind. And as more men arrived, two in suits and the remainder in crimson uniforms, she discovered that they too, seemed to have no draw for her mind. The thundering focused on the others but seemed to just ignore the Queen and her retinue.

Enzo laid a reassuring hand on Kat's arm, "don't fret, we'll get to the bottom of this."

She smiled at him, grateful, even though she knew better. Something was very wrong here, and she had dragged her family right into it. Then she noticed the young woman with more curiosity than sense still sat in her chair.

"You should really go now," Kat advised her.

But the woman shook her head, no.

"Why?" She asked confused.

"Because you're important to Will," Mary said simply.

"Will is here?" She asked, alarmed.

Mary nodded.

Katia put her head in her hands. She couldn't breathe, couldn't think. She was going to do it, her worst fears realized. She was going to destroy Will Kelly, and in some way she could never have imagined.

Chapter 10

The elevator doors opened into the psychomanteum.

As they had been instructed, the guests veered sharply to the right, immediately encountering the group from the neighboring car. Directing them to the right as Will had instructed, the people funneled all the new arrivals in one direction. The new devotees had arrived from the elevators nearly a quarter-hour early, and so no pages were there to greet them. The thinned numbers of guards in crimson were quickly overwhelmed as they attempted in vain to stem the human tide.

In the chaos that resulted, Will slipped to the left and around a corner. With a mental blueprint in his mind, he made his way toward the séance chambers. As he walked past another gaudy alcove, his eyes began to burn. Peeking in he found the body of a porter with a fancy hatpin through his skull. Carla.

His walk became a run. He rounded the corner and came face-to-face with two more red clad men guarding double doors. This was the room.

"Has a small Spanish woman entered this room?"

While his disguise might fool a human, he only confirmed to the men that they had found the human agent their general was seeking.

The taller of the two stepped slightly forward, his expression blank. "Of course, she's right inside."

The two men opened the door and ushered Will in.

"Kat?" Will spotted her immediately. "Where's Carla?"

"Will?" Mary responded to his voice from behind one of the dark chairs.

"Mary?" Will was afraid of this. A worst-case scenario.

"Enough." The Queen commanded.

The taller man behind Will bowed slightly. "My Queen, the human agent you have been seeking." He indicated Will.

Will was still trying to make sense of what he was seeing when his cover was so carelessly discarded. Now he had to figure out how to get himself, plus four others untangled from this situation. He didn't want to hurt anyone, but he would if the moment called for it. There were more red jackets in the room than he had bullets in his colt, but he'd take out as many as he could before they overwhelmed him.

"I am a detective, I'm looking for Carla Rios, I believe she means harm to Miss Katia Santaro. She has already killed one of your men."

The queen looked legitimately surprised by the fact but not overly concerned.

"She was here," the Queen said, "and she did intend harm to Miss Santoro. But it has been dealt with. Now I suppose you, as well, will have to be dealt with."

It should have stunned him, made him question if he had heard her correctly, but it failed. Will was already on alert so when the two men behind him tried to seize his arms, the agent stepped back between them. He pulled his arms free and shoved the two men into the room ahead of him, drawing the Colt out in a smooth, practiced fashion.

"Alright, Gallo, Enzo help the ladies out of the room." Will instructed.

Before either of the men could rise, Os'Fil stepped forward. He raised Carla's small, old-fashioned pistol in a single smooth motion and leveled it at Will.

The tension increased.

Will's thumb rested near the hammer of his Colt and he met the Outsider's gaze with a faint smile. He cocked his head as if he was sharing a helpful tip.

"You ever shoot a man?" He asked, coolly.

Os'Fil did not respond to the taunt. Not even a blink.

Will gave a humorless smile, eyes flicking briefly to the pistol. "Harder than it looks. Farther away you are, more likely you are to miss. That little antique you have there. You might scratch my ribs—if you're a very good shot."

Os'Fil now tilted his head to the side, he seemed to process Will's words. Then, he moved. Not toward Will, but toward Katia. He closed the distance smoothly, stepping behind her chair. The barrel of the pistol leveled at the back of her head through the wooden rails.

Will froze. Katia closed her eyes slowly, realizing that Will was now trapped.

I'Pa turned toward her general, a flicker of shock flashed across her calm facade. But she held her tongue. She understood what

Os'Fil had done, because it worked. Will's arm slackened and his lips parted, and for a moment he didn't say anything.

Then, quietly, he said, "Alright."

He dropped the pistol to the floor. The Colt landed with a heavy clunk, and he stared at it as if the weapon had betrayed him.

"Seize them all." Os'Fil ordered.

With a rustle of fabric, red liveried men took hold of Will, Gallo and Enzo, and pulled them away from the table and their queen. Dul'Sa sat at the table and lit a pipe. The Herald found a chair along the wall, away from the humans, and made himself small. Then the crown arrived.

A crimson-uniformed man stepped into the room carrying the curious device. It was not for ceremony, not anymore, and it was certainly not holy.

It was a machine.

Designed by Andrei Fischer himself, before Dul'Sa's habitation had slowly unspooled the man's brilliance into obedient madness followed by death. Crafted in those last, final lucid months, when genius and obsession had not yet faded and passed. It looked like something feral—baroque spirals of lacquered bone and horn, branching like a corrupted halo—but it served a chillingly pragmatic function.

Outsider technicians had aided him, and the entire, twisted thing was covered in the carapaces of their dead. It now conducted and focused more energy than even Fischer had envisioned, but sadly, where most humans were concerned, that added up to little. And so, the crown had found renewed purpose under the Outsider's scientists.

Inside its gnarled structure, a core was built—a micro-chamber, sealed and lined in a substance more suitable to maintain the Outsiders' alien environment. It protected the Outsider within from Earth's noxious atmosphere during the brief, unbearable seconds between hosts. A miniature, and therefore more limited version of the larger cylinders on the highest floor that humans were placed in for infestation.

Few had seen it used; its efficacy was still an open question. It was created for emergencies, when the transfer must take place outside the dedicated chamber at Eventide's pinnacle. Or so they said. I'Pa thought they just wanted to play with human technology.

But now she would put their labor to the test, this was just such an emergency they had designed it for.

"Carry it carefully," I'Pa ordered, "do not damage the chamber."

The crown was not bedecked in jewels. Nor gilded with gold. No velvet.

It was a wound made into an object. A piece of a place that should not exist in this time or place. It was alien, and every human could feel its corruption like heat from a fire.

I'Pa glided forward and took Enzo's seat at Katia's right. Katia turned to regard the Queen slowly. Their eyes met. One pair human—wide, exhausted, but alight with something bright and mad and alive. The other held something deeper. Older. Simpler.

"Now," I'Pa instructed her warrior. "Place it on me."

The crimson-clad man stepped forward, arms outstretched, holding the crown before him. Katia recoiled at the sight of it. It looked less like a crown and more like a living threat. Coiled horns, fossilized tendrils, the gleam of ancient resin folded into a lattice that hummed in frequencies that made her skin crawl.

A breath away from the Queen's scalp, the warped coils seemed to twitch. Then the crown settled. Not like metal on flesh, but more akin to an acetabula from a giant kraken's tentacle. And for a moment…silence.

Then, from beneath the crown came the filaments.

They were slow at first—slender tendrils of darkness slipping from beneath the crown like curls of ink dispersing in water. They drifted upward, then downward, then sideways, as if unsure of the air. Wisps of shadow that were without weight, impossibly delicate, almost invisible—until they began to thicken by numbers.

More of them emerged, weaving in the air like spider silk stirred by breath. They clung to her scalp, her jawline, her throat. They did not move so much as they spread. Like an infestation.

Katia leaned away but did not rise. She could not. She was the reason they were there, her family, friends and even a stranger. She would face whatever fate had in store for them. All of them.

Queen Carlotta's body went rigid. A full spasm, sharp and cruel. Her back arched slightly, shoulders twitching. One of her eyes fluttered, then rolled—pale white exposed to the shadows above. Her lips parted as if to speak, but no sound emerged.

And then, she collapsed.

The man pulled the crown free of Carlotta's head with visible effort. Once it was free, her body toppled from the chair with a dull, lifeless thud. The corpse landed unceremoniously, limbs splayed and graceless, one arm twisted beneath her back, her jaw slack. The crown left its mark, a dark ring around her brow—like soot from a snuffed flame.

To her credit Katia did not react when the body tumbled to the thick carpet. But a deep pit opened inside her when she realized what they intended. All eyes turned to her as the man with the crown approached her. It was too late to avoid her fate, but she would still fight it every step.

The man stepped closer, the wicked looking crown held reverently. Will struggled against his captors. A blow struck his side; a boot forced him down. Gallo bellowed, Enzo broke free for a breath before he, too, was tackled and pinned to the dark red floor.

The crown descended and kissed her brow. And the filaments came again, and Kat's terror reached its zenith.

"I'm sorry Will," she cried out as the threads of darkness spread across her eyes, "I'm so sorry."

Kat reached up in panic and pulled masses of the shadowy tendrils away from her face, but they just wound around her fingers and hands causing them to go cold and numb. She wanted to apologize to Gallo and Enzo as well, poor Mary too, but she ran out of time before her true suffering began.

Some of the smokey tendrils drove downward into her scalp. They writhed beneath her skin, slick with something more than just blood. They burrowed with vicious intent. Katia's jaw clenched. Her back arched and red-clad men seized her arms in a vice as she fought the crown. A whimper became a scream as the fine black threads vanished into her skull like worms into soft earth.

A line of blood trickled from beneath the crown. Then another. Crimson rivulets raced down her cheek and neck, gathering in her collar. The threads were piercing her skull, working their way along a long-healed suture from birth. With surprising strength, the darkness forced the bone open to expose her brain under the crown. A soft cracking sound echoed faintly, sickening and surreal.

Her body was writhing and twisting in agony. Fingers curled into claws, knuckles cracking from stress. A sound began deep in her throat, building. The Angel screamed again—a long, painful wail as her body was violated.

The sound was enough to drive Will into action. Gathering his legs, he twisted and drove into the man holding his left arm. The guard let a choked cry as he slammed into the heavy table, the impact had no effect on the furniture. The second guard reclaimed Will's right arm.

There were too many for him to handle alone, but Kat's cry caused a split-second decision. Will struck swift and hard on the second man. His left fist struck the man in the throat, incapacitating and possibly even killing him. But Will ignored that possibility focused solely on reaching Katia and tearing the crown from her head.

Then he felt an iron grip on his left arm. Os'Fil had moved to intercept Will, and he was strong. Much stronger than Will had judged. But he was also off-balance, and Will rolled his arm under and grabbed Os'Fil's arm in return. Then he leaned into the general's shoulder and twisted, forcing Os'Fil down and striking his head soundly on the black wood. The Outsider's host crumpled to the floor.

Katia grew quiet.

Everyone stilled, watching the young woman. What they saw, none of them expected.

The Angel grinned widely, maniacally, she brought her hands up before her eyes and toyed with the strands of shadow. A predatory tittering welled up inside her.

"Something's wrong," Dul'Sa stated.

Will couldn't agree more, and he retrieved the Colt. If Kat was permanently harmed by any of this, he'd tear this building to the ground. His eye fell on the man who had just spoke. Will recognized Andrei Fischer from photographs. He cocked the hammer, deciding the building's owner would be a good place to start getting answers.

Kat grew still once more. Her lips parted. Her mouth worked soundlessly, stiffly. Once. Twice and again.

Then she smiled. Not a maniacal one this time, but a triumphant one.

"I believe," came the voice, velvet-wrapped and commanding, "that the ritual is complete."

The words rolled from Katia's mouth smoothly, naturally, but Will felt none of the woman he loved in that voice.

"Will," Enzo asked, "what just happened?"

"Good question, Enzo," Will replied, cocking the Colt's hammer. Gallo said something to Enzo in Italian.

"Be still and the Angel will not be harmed," I'Pa said through Kat's mouth. "Test me and I will ravage her mind before I kill her."

That caught the humans off guard. They looked at each other in bewilderment. No one knew how to respond.

"That seemed…unusual," Dul'Sa said, coming closer to the Queen, but keeping a vigilant eye on the human with the gun.

"Yes," I'Pa confirmed, "this human's mind is remarkable, but—confusing. She has…boundaries. Areas that I must force myself into. I have never encountered anything like this."

"Nor have I," the Emissary confirmed, "and I have no memory of anyone else speaking of such a thing."

It was a relatively small and select group of Outsiders that got to ride a human host. And as such, they shared experiences frequently. No humans have ever resisted habitation. How could they, with the Outsider in direct contact with the brain? Their choice was effectively bypassed.

Except this time for some reason. Dul'Sa, fascinated with anything related to humans, took a seat on the Queen's left.

"Is she still struggling?" The Emissary asked around the stem of his pipe. He wanted to reach out and touch I'Pa for a better examination but wisely knew better.

Will's confusion and anger reached a fever pitch. Noticing the first two guards he'd attacked were recovering, the agent physically propelled both men to the other side of the table. Os'Fil remained motionless. But with only one of the men down he still had only a tenuous edge. He had the gun, but they still had more men than he had bullets. He fell back on his law enforcement training.

"Alright," he motioned with his free hand toward Kat, "stand up, we're leaving."

I'Pa and Dul'Sa both ignored him.

"I don't think this is about me," the Queen explained, "these defenses must have taken years to erect."

"Mmmm, wonder what she was trying to keep out," the Emissary speculated around the pipe's mouthpiece. "Her energy output has dropped off precipitously."

"I know," she replied, "I don't understand that."

Will tried to gain control of the room again. This was only going to end his way as long they left now. Every moment they lingered in this room was more time for red coated reinforcements to arrive. He looked at Gallo and Enzo still being restrained.

"Release them now." He ordered.

The men stared back at him, but that was all.

"I will shoot you," he warned, raising the pistol at one of the men holding Enzo.

Again, they ignored his instructions. William marveled at life's ability to put one's feet at crossroads they could never have imagined even existed. He'd never found himself in such an absurd position, and what the hell was this situation? Unable to adequately assess the crisis, he turned to Mary to confirm she was unharmed. Shockingly, Mary nodded calmly amid the chaos, acknowledging her complete confidence in him. He was surprised to find that Mary's faith bolstered his morale.

"What has the human said?" Dul'Sa asked.

I'Pa's host shook her head.

"She is not here."

"Wait," the Herald spoke up, "I thought…did the transfer kill the human?"

"No, she lives," the Queen explained, "I simply cannot find her."

"Hmmm," Dul'Sa chewed on his pipe as he tried to conceive of some reason for the bizarre behavior.

"What is this?" I'Pa asked, then her voice grew more concerned. "Quickly! Remove the crown!"

The Emissary rose to do the task himself, but he could feel that it was already too late. The Angel's astonishing energy had returned, but in far greater abundance.

The maniacal grin returned. Then she screamed. Not Katia and not quite I'Pa, but a combination. A shared pain.

An Earth-shattering shriek tore through the chamber like a knife. It pitched too high, too long. A keening wail that vibrated in the bone. And then others began to scream.

The men in crimson suits.

The Herald.

Dul'Sa, inside the corpse of Andrei Fischer.

They all dropped to their knees, howling. Hands clutching heads. Backs arched. Mouths torn open. For a moment all was sound and confusion.

As swift as it started, the sound cut off. The afflicted people collapsed in heaps where they stood. The two men holding Gallo buried the poor man in a tangle of crimson limbs. Dul'Sa sagged in his chair, the pipe thumped to the carpet.

Kat's head slammed down on the table's unyielding surface. The crown cushioned the impact, shattering much of the twisting horns that formed it. Chitin and metal scattered across the table with enough force to strike the walls and force Mary to shield her face from the debris.

Will lifted her back and cradled her head, "Kat. Kat."

Her left eye fluttered open.

It was red—blooming with crimson—but behind it, he saw her. Kat.

A single tear cut down her cheek as she smiled at him.

"It was softer than I expected, Will," she whispered.

And then her eyes fluttered shut and her muscles went slack. Her head fell against his chest.

"No—no, Kat—Kat!"

But there was no response.

Enzo untangled his father from their captor's bodies, then they joined Will at Kat's side. Will lifted the unconscious woman in his arms and stood.

Mary was still in her seat, halfway slumped to the floor, one hand clamped over her mouth. Her eyes were wide, vacant. She'd seen all of it—every horrifying moment.

Will turned, fury suppressed beneath the need to get them all to safety. He carried Katia like a bride around the table, stopping at the shocked woman.

"Now, Mary," he said, calm but cutting, "we're leaving. Now."

Mary flinched as she snapped out of her shock. She rose, legs shaking, and followed.

In the corridor Mary removed her heels to keep up with Will's swift pace.

Chapter 11
I'Pa's Fall: The Gate Closes

"I believe that the ritual is complete."

The humans spoke to each other, I'Pa paid little attention to them, but they inevitably intruded upon her work.

"Be still and the Angel will not be harmed," I'Pa said through Kat's mouth. "Test me and I will ravage her mind before I kill her."

That shut them up.

I'Pa was disappointed. And equally perplexed. The energy emissions that had dazzled them from this host had vanished. The same thing happened with every host the moment human consciousness passed. Some emergent property simply disappeared from the human's being. But this was not the case here. Katia lived, I'Pa could feel her, though she could not locate the human's consciousness. The Queen was left unsure of how to proceed. This was the crux of the Outsider's shortcomings, ignorance.

A functioning brain should be all that is required to generate the power that sustained her people, no consciousness should be necessary. It defied all reason that something as unnecessary as intelligence should be responsible for the energy the Queen sought.

After all, the Outsiders themselves had intelligence, yet emitted no such power as the humans did. True, they were from two very different universes, but Outsider science had ruled out any such interactions being the origin of the power. Research continued, of course, and one day they would answer the question.

And so, even in the face of insurmountable evidence pointing to an emergent quality from the humans themselves, the Queen refused to entertain the concept.

But this made no sense; a functioning brain should be all that is required. And so, even in the face of insurmountable evidence—I'Pa's operations drawing in normal humans to harvest—the Outsiders remained certain that they had just missed something. And one day, they would discover that overlooked method to reactivate the generator inside the human.

I'Pa, who knew humans better than any Outsider, found this theory inconceivable. The Queen had little respect for humanity, aside from its quality of providing her race with life-giving energy. In her assessment, humans were the sole reason her race existed at its current state of advancement. Not that the energy in any way altered them physically, but it had offered incomparable sustenance that allowed her kind to undertake endeavors other than endless scavenging.

Endeavors that eventually bore fruit such as science and culture. I'Pa liked science, it was straightforward and predictable. Rational. Humans were not rational creatures. They did not think in straight lines, at least not entirely. Human minds moved in oblique and still mysterious ways.

Even Fischer, who the Queen had personally ridden herself, could not explain how he built the Eventide. The discussion always ended with the same inexplicable concept: *inspiration*.

Much like the foreign abstraction they called *hope* that generated so much of the energy she desired.

Or predestination.

"That seemed…unusual," she heard Dul'Sa say.

"Yes," she replied, "this human's mind is remarkable, but—confusing. She has…boundaries. Areas that I must force myself into. I have never encountered anything like this."

Many Outsiders experienced some anomolies when a human was first taken as a host. The human was always afraid, even if they invited the inhabitation. Here, the Queen was having to force her way past barrier after barrier as she searched for the human's self.

"Nor have I," the Emissary answered, "and I have no memory of anyone else speaking of such a thing. Is she still struggling?"

I'Pa could not think of a way to suitably describe the experience.

"I don't think this is about me," the Queen explained, "these defenses must have taken years to erect."

"Mmmm, wonder what she was trying to keep out," the Emissary speculated around the pipe's mouthpiece. "Her energy output has dropped off precipitously."

"I know," she lied, "I don't understand that."

"What has the human said?" Dul'Sa asked.

I'Pa's host shook her head. She could not keep this from the Emissary; she would be honest about that point at least. Though Dul'Sa would likely draw the same conclusions as her about the energy being tied to the human's self rather than the physical brain.

"She is not here."

"Wait," this from the Herald, "I thought…did the transfer kill the human?"

"No, she lives," the Queen admitted, "I simply cannot find her."

"Hmmm," Dul'Sa chewed on his pipe as he tried to conceive of some reason for the bizarre behavior.

That was when I'Pa first noticed the tremor. The inside of a human is a noisy place, especially for a creature that senses and communicates by vibrations. The heart alone could deafen one if they were not trained to cancel out its robust pulsation. This new sound was different, unbroken.

A constant thrumming that seemed to come from all around. Not uncommon in and of itself; after all she was sitting in the cup of a liquid-filled chamber. But this felt more…intentional. The Queen could swear she detected faint tremors in the vibration that she could almost understand, as if it were trying to communicate.

I'Pa pushed deeper, seeking any sign of the human's mind while splitting her focus to monitor the strange manifestation. The *growing* manifestation she realized. The Queen stopped her intrusion. It was reacting to her progress, increasing in intensity the farther she pushed into the human's defenses.

I'Pa realized too late that she had dismantled too many of Kat's mental walls by this point, and what was left dissolved before

the ever-grinding machine. It swept over the hive-queen like a force of nature.

"What is this?" I'Pa asked. Vibrations dusted her body lightly, washing over her as if something was examining the Queen. Then the walls came down completely. She felt the human's mind light up with an onslaught of the energy she sought. "Quickly! Remove the crown!"

But it was far too late by then. She should have ordered the crown removed earlier, but she had been certain that she was in control of the situation. This was something I'Pa had never encountered, so she could not accurately name what she witnessed, but she came close. Chaos.

It was a maelstrom of emotion and broken thoughts. With all of Kat's carefully constructed mental walls effectively breached, her mind fell into madness. She had managed to hide from the Queen, but madness found her at once and consumed Katia whole. Understanding passed from her like a soft breeze and Kat knew no more.

The chaotic assault on I'Pa's mind was a grindstone. As it began to drive I'Pa mad, she had a fleeting moment to reflect all she had done, and all that would come from her mistake. Her detractors had been right. The power was too great, and the crown amplified the power to the point that it burned her chitin armor.

Predestination.

It was her last thought before the energy that washed over her body reduced the hive-queen to ash. I'Pa died before she could fully lose her mind. But she wouldn't be alone.

The crown did its job well—but it had limitations. The

excessive amount of energy flooding the device quickly overwhelmed its capacity. Energy that could not be transferred to the building's core then escaped along the magnetic field lines formed by the crown. This created two lobes of lethal energy that spun several times a second. The waves passed over the Outsiders reducing them to ash just as it had done to their queen.

The sphere of energy expanded nearly a hundred feet in every direction. The Eventide's exotic antenna, housed at the building's core, amplified this effect on a scale that spanned nearly seventeen miles. The entire expeditionary force of the Outsiders was erased in moments. They were the lucky ones.

The channel between worlds, once carefully controlled to allow a steady stream of human-harvested energy, became a torrent. Or more aptly, a ray of death. The hives, interconnected for efficiency, as they had been for time immemorial, were formed from the bodies of their dead. The hives themselves and their connecting tunnels conducted the energy. The great constructs were now linked in tragedy. Six million strong. Compartments of life and labor and queens—all fed by the lattice of energy they'd harvested from the humans.

And now it betrayed them.

The energy struck the primary lattice-node and slivered out in all directions, faster than thought. Entire strata of hive workers—nurse broods, warriors, engineers—evaporated mid-task. Their screams didn't even have time to reach their queens.

The power surged, pulsing where it entered their universe, creating repeated shock waves that rocketed through the chlorine-heavy atmosphere faster than sound. Cell walls blackened. Antennae liquefied. Storage caverns exploded inward, their egg-sacs bubbling in the residual heat. The songs of six million queens fell silent.

And then it ended. Just silence. A part of their world was reduced to black detritus, but the whole of their world changed forever.

The decision to deploy the Hive Killer was never actually a formal decision. The drones overseeing the device panicked, certain it was the end of their world. They launched the great sphere of destruction in what they believed would be their final act.

The bomb was larger than a hive, so it found its target easily: the inverted point of the Eventide, where the psychomanteum's mirrored fang stabbed their world like a thorn from a giant. The rupture that had made their empire fat and lazy.

Now, a gaping wound.

Despite its great size the Hive-Killer penetrated the membrane with a scream of pressure imbalance between the two worlds. Then it blossomed in a great blinding flash and a single, massive shock wave. The Eventide was no more.

Chapter 12

The descent in the elevator was silent and tense. No one knew what to say, nor were they brave enough to begin asking questions. Will focused his attention on Kat, concerned that she hadn't regained consciousness.

Then he turned to Mary, "I'm sorry I dragged you into this mess Mary. How are you holding up?"

Mary mustered a sincere smile for her friend. She reached out and squeezed Will's arm.

"I'll be fine, Will, thanks to you." She looked at Katia, "is she going to be alright?"

Will shrugged, uncertain at this time, but worry was in his eyes and all over his face, as much as he tried to hide it. Mary felt her heart break in a different way this time.

A sound began to build then. An ordinary sound, harmless and mechanical, like any other elevator in Manhattan. But the hair on the back of Will's neck began to stand up as it intensified.

Then the sound changed, a roar swelling from somewhere above, too vast and unnatural to belong to anything good. The sound rose in pitch as the bomb began chewing away at the soft metal hidden in the building's core. The Outsiders had run extensive experiments on the strange metal, and the Hive-Killer put that knowledge to good use.

Then came the pressure, barely noticeable at first, a dull bloom behind the eyes. Then they felt their ears pop. Mary gasped, clutching her temples. Enzo staggered into the corner, eyes wide. Gallo went down to a knee. And Kat, held tight in Will's arms, stiffened from the discomfort. Her body shivered in his grasp.

Will wanted off this elevator, but he knew better than anyone how congested the stairs were. True there might not be any red coated men on the lower floors, but then again, he did not know that for a fact. Eventually there would be police; Will had no doubt there were multiple fatalities. And he could not explain anything that he'd just witnessed, so he put it from his mind and focused on getting out of the building unseen and alive.

He scanned the elevator's console for inspiration. He looked at Gallo. "The alley—how did you get from the alley to the mezzanine?"

Gallo shrugged helplessly, but Enzo's voice came sharp. "I remember every step."

Without waiting, Will snapped his boot forward, striking the mezzanine button. After a long moment the elevator halted with a jolt. The lift doors opened to confused porters who jumped out of Will's way as he burst from the lift.

"This way," Enzo called over the music and merriment. Guests continued with their revelry, unaware of the bizarre occurrences going on throughout the upper floors.

The others followed, weaving around knots of people as they made their way toward the building's rear access. At last, they arrived at a set of double doors marked 'STAFF ONLY'. The crimson coat gained them unfettered access to the Eventide, and they were soon passing out of the building and into the alley.

A sound, something between a howling and a grinding drew their attention upward. At the tower's peak the Hive-Killer eroded the metal and stone and compressed it into a liquid. That liquid was mixed with elements within the bomb to create fuel. At the same time, the spinning device sucked in air at a tremendous rate, sorting and compressing the oxygen to create an aerosolized fuel bomb.

It represented the height of Outsider technology and the bomb worked, but not perfectly. The Outsiders' knowledge of the human universe was still very limited, so many of their calculations were conducted with incomplete or erroneous data. While intended to consume the entire soft-metal core of the Eventide for fuel, the bomb reached capacity and detonated by the time it reached the thirty-ninth floor.

The explosion was over in a fraction of a second. In one moment, Will felt the air pulling on him reach a crisis and then there was flash of light and a deafening blast wave that lifted all of them off their feet. He kept Kat close, and her added weight knocked the wind from him when he impacted the road. Unable to hear, they were unaware of the debris falling around them until a chunk of masonry landed near Gallo's head.

Will struggled to his feet and yelled, pointless as it was, for the others to run. They raced away from the building darting into the first cover they found. A sheltered entryway of an adjacent building. When their hearing returned, they wished it hadn't.

The sound of shrieking screams filled the night. Later it would be revealed that they had heard the super-heated metal girders of the Eventide cooling rapidly in the bitter winter air. But for those that had been there, and had witnessed the cataclysm, some maintained that it was the sounds of the dead crying out in victory, their vengeance on the occultists complete.

Will stared up at the Eventide, its upper floors, the psychomanteum, were gone. The steel and glass were bent and twisted as if the building's crown had been snuffed like a candle by an angry god.

Will felt Kat stirring in his arms and glanced down. Her eyes were open, looking into his own. He smiled, not realizing just how close he'd come to losing her until he saw her alive.

"Hello, beautiful," he leaned over her with a smile that belied his exhausted appearance. "How do you feel?"

Her voice was a whisper.

"Something's wrong, Will. I feel...*nothing.*" Ω

We hope you enjoyed these three dark tales, each sparked by a prompt from our **STORYFORGE** universe. *Frights From the Forge* is our first fiction collection, but it all began with the books below: writing prompt companions designed to help you create your own horror, fantasy, science fiction and more.

Scan the QR code to explore the full series. Every book is forged with imagination, and if this one lit a fire in you, we'd be grateful for your honest review.

Advanced Horror Writing
ASIN: BOCZ3QY2BF

Advanced Horror Writing Book Two
ASIN: BOD5RQZPSC

Advanced Horror Writing Book Three
ASIN: BODHVJ8Q85

Advanced Horror Writing Book Four
ASIN: BOFBKXQNK1

Advanced Fantasy Writing
ASIN: B0D3D5WS11

Advanced Fantasy Writing Book Two
ASIN: B0D76BGHBQ

Advanced Fantasy Writing Book Three
ASIN: B0DL3ZFZKL

Advanced Fantasy Writing Book Four
ASIN: B0FLD5C1B4

Advanced Science Fiction Writing
ASIN: B0D4HQLMV1

**Advanced Science Fiction Writing
Book Two**
ASIN: B0CZ3QY2BF

**Advanced Science Fiction Writing
Book Three**
ASIN: B0DNST54FT

Advanced Special Character Writing
ASIN: B0D8HRFH27

**Advanced Special Character Writing
Book Two**
ASIN: B0DXFWFG4B

ST✪RYFORGE

FRIGHTS FROM THE FORGE

THANKS FOR STEPPING INTO THE DARK WITH US.

We hope you enjoyed *Frights From the Forge* and that its strange shadows and sinister sparks lit up your imagination in all the right ways.

The **STORYFORGE** series doesn't stop here. Alongside eerie tales and haunting novellas, we've created companion books packed with writing prompts for horror, fantasy, science fiction and more—designed to spark your creativity and challenge your storytelling skills. And don't forget, all our prompts are completely free for you to use in your work, but please reference prompt books only, not these full stories.

Scan the QR code below to explore the full collection. We've got plenty more frights, and inspiration, in the fire.

STORYFORGE

a book by **Odd&Mollie Supply** LLC © 2026

www.ingramcontent.com/pod-product-compliance
Lightning Source LLC
Chambersburg PA
CBHW060401260626
47160CB00006B/2397